MW00326113

THE WAY YOU ARE

A Carolina Connections Novel

SYLVIE STEWART

Rolling Hearts Press

COPYRIGHT

In accordance with the U.S. Copyright Act of 1976, the scanning, uploading, and electronic sharing of any part of this book without the permission of the publisher constitute unlawful piracy and theft of the author's intellectual property. If you would like to use material from the book (other than brief quotations for review purposes), prior written permission must be obtained by the author who can be contacted at sylvie@sylviestewartauthor.com. Thank you for your support of the author's rights.

This book is a work of fiction. Names, characters, places, and incidents are products of the author's imagination or are used fictitiously. Any resemblance to actual persons, living or dead, events, or locales is entirely coincidental.

First Edition: 2018

Copyright © 2018 Sylvie Stewart

Edited by Heather Mann

ISBN: 978-1-947853-08-9

ALSO BY SYLVIE STEWART

Full-On Clinger (*Love on Tap* novella/prequel)

Booby Trapped (Asheville short)

Crushing on Casanova (Asheville short)

Taunted (Asheville short)

Love on Tap Series - coming 2022

To Maria and Jeff
for knowing the importance of raising a nice guy

Chapter One

COJONES ARE MY LIFE

RETT

"Hey, Blue! Get off your knees—you're blowin' the game!"

My head snapped to the right at the unexpected taunt. Not that fans heckling the ump were anything unusual, but this comment came with a loud, feminine voice attached to it. I shifted in my seat to get a better look at the next section over, but a large man wielding his concessions stash of hot dogs and beer blocked my view.

The insult wasn't a bad one, I had to admit. I was never one to heckle the ump myself—especially this guy, Gleeson. The players, on the other hand, were fair game all day long. I just never wanted to get booted from the stadium and miss any of the game. And pissing the umpire off was just the way to find your ass watching the game from behind the gates.

2 • SYLVIE STEWART

"Come on, Franks! You got this!" I cupped my hands around my mouth, not that the Guardians pitcher could hear me anyway. My voice couldn't carry nearly as far as the chick over in section 104. I groaned as the batter caught a piece of Franks' curveball and hauled ass all the way to second. Turned out Gavin and Emerson weren't missing much. My best friend and his girl had joined me for the first game of this double-header with the Charleston Kings, but they'd begged off before the second game started—no doubt to go fuck each other's brains out. At least I wouldn't be home to hear it through the walls in case they decided to head back to Gavin's and my place.

At the rate those two were going, though, I was guessing it would be just my place before too long. I could see the writing on the wall. Everyone I knew was pairing up and it was starting to make me a bit paranoid. But I was being smart. Careful. The next time I got involved, it would be with the right girl for the right reasons. I was done letting a nice pair of tits turn me into a walking hard-on with the word "doormat" tattooed on it.

Shit. That was a horrible mental image. I looked down at my crotch and silently apologized to my dick.

The Kings' next batter hit a line drive to left field and got himself on first, but the inning turned over when he got cocky and drew the final out trying to steal second. He was gonna find himself back with the rookies if he didn't check his judgment.

"That's the way, Horner! Keep it up and you'll be scoring bigtime later tonight!" There came the shouting again, this time directed at the Guardians' new second baseman—some big dude named Troy Horner. He turned to the stands with a flash of white teeth while our shortstop, Joey Martel, looked in the same direction and scowled.

Interesting. Looked like someone woke up on the wrong side of the bed this morning.

This time, when I searched for the source of the comments, I spotted her. Though she wasn't yelling anymore, it could only have been her. The girl looked about twenty and was decked out in a green and gold Guardians jersey that swamped her small frame. Long black hair cascaded down her back from beneath the bright green ballcap, and huge sunglasses sat on her small face. I felt my lips curve up at the sight. For someone so tiny, she sure could make a racket.

Looking around the stands, I noticed the crowd had begun to thin out—not unusual for a double header this early in the season. But where had this chick been for the first game? I knew I would have noticed her. Looked like I'd have more entertainment than anticipated this evening.

To me, there's nothing better than a Saturday at the ball park. Baseball is in my blood, thanks to my Pop and Grandpop. As a kid, it was my dream to make it to the majors, but I learned early on that you had to possess coordination and actual skill at playing the game to make it anywhere. In a word, I suck. But that never stopped me from being the biggest fan out there. Ask me anything about the game and I can tell you. Some of us, like Gavin, were meant to play. Others were meant to revere, obsess, and bask in the simple perfection of the game. That's me, all the way.

I took a sip of my beer and watched my team—well, one of my teams—prepare to bat. The Greensboro Guardians are a double A minors team, but the fact that their stadium is a fifteen-minute drive from my place makes them the team I watch most often. Then there's the Knights and the Bulls, coming from Charlotte and Durham respectively. Those guys are triple A and are only a couple hours away—best $25 a guy can spend to see some big names throwing the ball in a local stadium. But, hell, give me any game and I'll be there. In fact, Emerson's brother plays for North High School and I watch him at least once a week. That kid has a future, I'll tell you that.

Our first player came up to bat, and I found myself holding my breath, waiting to see if the little heckler would speak up. A glance in her direction showed her attention riveted to the field. Damn, that was my kind of girl. The Kings' pitcher threw a fastball, catching our batter off guard. I sighed, and sure enough, there came the shouting.

"Come on, ump! That was low! This is baseball, not bowling!"

I smiled to myself and shook my head. This girl was asking for it.

The next batter connected right in the sweet spot and hauled ass until he slid safely into second.

"It's okay, pitcher! At least your mom still loves you!"

Several snickers sounded from around me, including a couple Kings fans. It seemed nobody was immune to her taunts.

Without thinking, I grabbed my beer and rose from my seat. Then I shuffled my way up the aisle to the concourse level before making my way over to section 104. Nobody was checking tickets, as there was no point this late in the day. She was about fifteen rows down and all I could see was the back of her head covered in that green hat and dark, shiny hair. I forced my attention to the field again. The Guardians just had the one player on second, and that new guy, Horner, was up at bat—the same guy she'd promised some post-game action to. Before I even knew what I was doing, I found myself shouting in my loudest voice.

"This guy hasn't driven anybody home since junior prom!"

A few chuckles sounded around me, and then she turned. She halted when she singled me out and I stared at her until she lowered her giant sunglasses and glared daggers my way. I couldn't stop myself. I burst out laughing and didn't miss the tiny twitch of her lips before she swung her head back around to the action on the field.

Another out and a couple more vigorous insults thrown at the ump from the glaring heckler, and I spotted two security guards taking the stairs down in her direction. Shit. Not that I didn't see this coming, but I knew how I'd feel if I got kicked out.

I found myself trailing the guards down the aisle and slipping into the row behind the girl as they shuffled their way into the row in front of her.

"Ma'am, I'm afraid we're going to have to ask you to gather your belonging and follow us."

"What do you mean? Why?"

"Ma'am, you've been heckling the umpire all evening."

She shrugged her small shoulders in that huge jersey and made no move to get up. "I call 'em as I see 'em. You can't fault me for that."

"Actually, we can. Listen," said the other guard. "Cheering is encouraged, but when you start using profanity and insulting the official's mother, we've got a problem."

I raised my hand to catch the guard's attention. "Sir." Three sets of eyes settled on me, one now stripped of the ridiculous sunglasses. "I believe the lady was referring to Gleeson's mother's china cabinet." They all looked at me as if I'd hit the beer concessions a bit too hard. I just shook my head and pressed on. "It's a common mistake. I imagine the cabinet, in fact, does have very large *drawers*—cajones." I mimed opening a drawer, still not sure why in the hell I was interfering. "It means drawers … you know, in Spanish." I eyed the girl, silently urging her to play along. I couldn't do all the work here.

She finally nodded and turned back to the guards with the fakest damn laugh I've ever heard. "Oh, you thought I was telling the ump his mom had bigger …" she pointed covertly to one of the guards' crotches. "… than he does?" Her head switched to a shake. "Oh, no. I'm a lady. I don't—"

I cut her off before she could add any more layers of bullshit. "Like I said, common mistake. The one you're thinking of is spelled with two Os." I smiled innocently and gave my beard a scratch.

The girl turned her head to face me again, biting her lips to keep from laughing. Once she schooled her features, she turned back to the guards. "Yes. I'm a furniture dealer. Mrs., uh, Gleeson is one of my best customers. What can I say? Cajones are my life." She put her hands out in a *what are ya gonna do* gesture. "Sorry for the confusion."

The guards' eyes passed back and forth between me and the troublemaker before settling firmly on her again. The closest one pointed a finger at her. "I don't want to hear another peep out of you unless it's singing someone's damn praises, you hear me?"

She put her hand up in what looked more like a Vulcan salute than any kind of gesture of Scout promise. "Yes, sir."

The second guard narrowed his eyes at both of us before the two uniformed men beat it back up the steps.

"Well, thanks for that." She turned again to me. I moved a seat over so she didn't have to strain her neck. Her normal speaking voice was silky and low, making me want to lean in to make sure I caught every word. "Nice save with the bullshit Spanish lesson."

I shook my head. "All true. I swear. I knew those years spent with Señora Berkovich would eventually pay off." I mimicked her ridiculous salute and she freaking giggled. The sound was like low-toned bells and my jeans were suddenly uncomfortably tight.

"I'm not sure if I believe you or not, but you saved me from missing my boyfriend's game so I'm giving you the benefit of the doubt."

Aaaaaand down went my semi.

"So, wait. How in the hell did both your cousin and your boyfriend end up on the same team? That's statistically impossible." I tried not to let the word boyfriend come out with a snarl. Not that I should have been surprised that a girl this cool was taken.

After turning around for the tenth time to make comments to me once the guards left, Liv Sun—short for Olivia because her mom had some weird preoccupation with the movie *Grease*—invited me to sit next to her for the rest of the game. We sipped our beers and talked baseball. She grew up with her cousin, the scowling shortstop from earlier, and had been indoctrinated into the sport from an early age. She confessed she generally cheered for whatever team her cousin was on at any given time, but her heart otherwise stayed with the Carolina teams. This pleased me beyond the point that could be deemed appropriate. I feared I was a bit screwed.

"Dumb luck, I guess. Troy and Joey were on their first minors team together and then each played for other farm teams for a couple years. They just happened to both end up in my neck of the woods this year, which works out well since I already have the jersey." She pulled at her shirt and I had to force my eyes from falling on her tits. "Although either one would jump at the chance to move up, obviously."

I nodded my understanding. These guys got shifted around a

lot, and it wasn't unheard of for a few to get plucked right from the double As for a spot in the majors mid-season.

Liv's eyes went back to the field where the pitcher was warming up. "I've known Troy since they first played together, but we didn't start dating until the end of last season. He and Joey got an off-season gig laying floors here in town, so they've both been around."

I nodded, as it was really the only polite thing to do. Troy Horner seemed like a decent player, if you liked second basemen, that is. *What? Everybody knows second base is where the biggest assholes gravitate.*

"So why were you heckling him earlier, by the way? He's on your team!" She gave me a dirty look.

I just laughed. "Maybe I felt bad for the Kings. None of their fans can heckle for shit."

She scrunched her nose and I noticed freckles dotting the golden skin of her nose and cheeks. "You're weird." Then she offered me some popcorn and smirked. "No wonder you're here alone."

"Hey," I protested. "It's not my fault my friends left." I gestured vaguely toward the concourse. "My buddy and his girl were here for the first game but they had to—" I stopped abruptly before I let the rest of that sentence escape.

Liv's brows creased. "Had to what?"

I looked to the field and tried to change the subject. "So, your cousin's having a good game."

"Not so fast!" She grabbed my wrist and a zing of electricity ran up toward my shoulder. Then she laughed. "Oh my God. They left to go screw! Ha!"

I broke out of my daze at her touch and saw her lips curve up into the widest and most beautiful smile I may have ever seen. Her laughter washed over me, and my heart thumped heavily in my chest. I forced a casual shrug and a grin back.

"Oh, I like your friends, Brett. And I like you. I can tell we're gonna be friends." She sat back in her seat and shoved a handful of popcorn in her mouth.

Fabulous. Just what I wanted. Another hot girl calling me her friend.

"Here. This way." Liv grabbed my arm again and pulled me behind her down the painted cinderblock hallway. I blinked at the brightness of the fluorescent lights. My arm was warm where she touched it, despite the chilled dampness of the stadium's lower level.

We approached the home team's locker room and Liv flashed her pass to the guard blocking the end of the hallway. He waved us past.

"Now, just to prepare you, Troy and Joey aren't expecting me to have someone with me, so I can't be responsible for their behavior."

As if on cue, the locker room door opened and Joey Martel stepped out, dressed in jeans and a polo, his hair wet from a shower. Before I could blink, he swept Liv up into a giant hug, engulfing her in his much larger frame. "Livvy!" He swung her back and forth, her legs dangling like a rag doll. When he finally set her back down, he looked her over from head to toe, taking in her Guardians gear and green Converse. "Nice! Looking great as always." He tweaked her ballcap. "We missed you at the first game. Could have used your big mouth to rattle the Kings."

She beamed back at him, the affection between the cousins

apparent. "I had to work this afternoon, it turned out. You guys looked great out there tonight, though!"

He nodded his dark head. "Thanks. One out of two—could have been better, could have been worse."

Liv seemed to remember me then and flashed a smile, gesturing for me to come closer.

"Joey, this is my friend Brett. He's a diehard Guardians fan, even if he doesn't dress like it." She shook her head at the decidedly plain gray Henley and ripped jeans I wore.

I raised a brow at her and approached her cousin. "Nice to meet you, man. Brett MacKinnon." I held out a hand.

He took it and smiled good-naturedly. "Joey Martel." Then to his cousin, "You guys work together?"

Liv laughed. "No. Actually, we just met today. Brett saved me from being ejected."

Joey coughed out a laugh. "I was wondering why you quieted down so early in the game."

"What's this about my girl getting ejected?" A deep voice sounded from behind us. Liv and I turned simultaneously to see Troy Horner standing in the locker room doorway. He was even bigger up close. His eyes were trained on me and there was not one hint of humor in them.

I wanted to roll my own eyes. This dude was about twice my size and could pound my head into the wall with a flick of his finger. Despite my best efforts, I never did pass the five-foot-eight mark. Genetics don't play around and they had me screwed from day one in the height department. Though I did my best to frequent the gym and work on my muscle mass, bench presses and Mr. Gold could only get you so far.

Liv threw herself into Troy's arms before he could move

another muscle. "Great game, baby!" She kissed him soundly on the mouth, and only then did his eyes leave me.

I guess it's kind of hard to visually pin someone to the wall when your tongue is down your girlfriend's throat.

Fuck. My. Life.

Chapter Two

WHATEVER THE QUESTION, SEX IS PROBABLY THE ANSWER

IV

There's something about a freshly showered man after a blatant display of athletic prowess that makes me horny. Okay, admittedly, it doesn't take a lot—I'm pretty much always horny. I've been told I'm the best kind of girlfriend in that respect. It's the other areas that apparently need some work.

"Troy!" I swatted at my hot boyfriend as he bodily lifted me from the ground and carried me around the corner from the locker room—and any eyewitnesses.

"Troy needs his girl to himself," he mumbled against my lips before sweeping his tongue into my mouth.

Okay, remember those other areas I was talking about? Yeah. Well this was one of them. I couldn't seem to keep my brain from doing a mental eyeroll at Troy's annoying habit of speaking about himself in the third person. I'm not gonna lie. It grated. Bigtime.

But it lost its effect as he expertly slanted his mouth to just the right angle and pulled my legs to wrap around his waist. Damn, he was good at this. I could feel his erection pressing against the seam of my jeans and began wondering where the closest horizontal surface was. I kissed him back with enthusiasm, feeling my inner muscles clench and my panties go damp.

I broke free to catch a much-needed breath, and Troy's tongue traced a path along my jaw and toward my ear. "Does Liv have what Troy needs?"

Ugh. I brought his mouth back to mine so he'd shut up and just kiss me for God's sake! Somewhere in the back of my mind I remembered that there were people waiting for us—people who probably wouldn't appreciate us fornicating in the hallway. Shit. I pulled back again and placed both hands on Troy's broad chest.

"Baby, we can't. We have to get back to Joey. And I want to introduce you to my friend."

Troy squeezed my asscheeks and dove back in. I swerved my head to the side, which did nothing to loosen his hold on me. My man was all man—and it didn't hurt that I was a shrimp. "I don't care about that dirtbag. Just you."

I smacked his chest. "Is that any way to talk about your teammate?!"

He pulled back again and scowled. "I was talking about your little buddy. Where'd you pick him up, anyway? Begging for change outside the stadium?"

I gasped and tried to jerk myself out of his hold, but he wouldn't let me go. He was acting like an asshole. Okay, so maybe Brett wasn't some clean-cut product of Alpha Phi Whatever, but he was a nice guy.

"Let me down, Troy." I glared at him and struggled some more. He winced when my movements jarred his right shoulder—the same one he'd been icing the last time he was in town—but he still didn't budge. I was starting to get pissed. "You don't even know the guy! He kept me from getting kicked out of the stadium!"

He laughed caustically. "I know everything I need to know. Dude's a freak."

That sent my head jerking back. I pushed harder on his chest, not giving a damn if he was sore, and he finally let me go, my Converse squeaking as they hit the sealed concrete floor. "Because he has a beard and a couple piercings? Judgmental much?"

Troy scoffed. "Whatever. I just don't like him."

I rolled my eyes for real this time. "Gee, Troy, you're so evolved." It was probably pointless of me to hope people wouldn't make judgments based solely on physical appearances. In fact, it was downright laughable. Growing up as a Chinese-American with two immigrant parents taught me that long ago. But I didn't have to like the fact that my boyfriend looked down on someone because of the way they chose to grow their facial hair or adorn their body. Last I checked, our generation was supposed to embrace diversity.

I guess Troy skipped that year in high school. He was probably busy crushing beer cans against his skull and getting laid. Troy was the poster boy for white American athletes with his close-cropped blond hair, strong nose, and sculpted muscles.

I turned my back to go and Troy grabbed my arm. "Hey, Liv! Calm the fuck down. I was just giving you a hard time." I glanced back at him and he was wearing a half smile. Hmm. I narrowed my eyes and crossed my arms.

"Oooh, Troy loves it when his Liv gets riled up."

Oh, for fuck's sake.

"Please tell me he doesn't talk about his penis that way," Haley groaned over the phone. Then she lowered her voice about ten octaves. "Troy Junior loves Liv's little pussy cat."

I couldn't keep the laughter from bubbling up my throat as I unlocked my apartment door. "I guess I should count myself lucky on that score. I honestly don't think I could handle it."

"From the stories I've heard, you've been *handling it* quite well."

I gasped in fake outrage. "You're one to talk! How is your little project going, anyway?" My best friend was on a mission to seduce her next-door neighbor, a hot young college professor who didn't seem to know she existed—a point that made me dislike him on principle.

"Still nothing." Haley sighed. "Well, he did say 'excuse me' when he stepped on my foot in the elevator this morning."

I set my bag on the armchair in my living room and frowned at the dismay in her voice. "Hales." My tone spoke volumes.

"I know. I know. If he doesn't like me, it's his loss."

"Damn straight!"

"But he's so cute. And those glasses. Uhn."

I bit my lip and tried not to laugh. My girl loved those nerd-boys.

"Okay. Calm your ovaries. When I'm in town next weekend, we'll figure out a way to lure the man from his nerd den."

"Hey!" She protested.

"What? You know me."

"Yeah, yeah. Whatever." Her tone switched up and I could hear her opening a bottle over the line. "So tell me about this guy you met." She sounded way too interested. Haley was terrible at lying so it was no secret to me that she wasn't overly fond of Troy. It wasn't like I planned on marrying the guy, though, so it didn't bother me too much. Troy and I were more about fun, sex, and baseball. I wasn't ready to think about the whole marriage and kids thing.

"Ha! You'd probably love him, come to think of it. He's around your height, he's got brown hair that's a little too long, and a beard. Oh! And he has ear plugs and at least two tattoos I'm aware of." I followed Haley's example and pulled a bottle of Childress from the refrigerator.

"Hmm. Interesting. What does he do for a living? Do you know?"

"We didn't really get around to that. He seems smart, though. And funny."

"Does he now? And he loves baseball? Sounds more like your type, Livvy," Haley taunted.

"Shut up. He's just a nice guy. I could use a new friend—especially since you up and ditched me!" I liked giving my BFF a hard time, but I was actually really proud of her. She'd just moved to Wilmington to take a job at a veterinary practice there and it was a pretty big deal.

"What can I say? The animals needed me. And the money ain't half bad either." She snickered. "But, seriously, you should hang out with this guy. It sounds like you have a lot in common, and if you're left with just Troy and Joey to keep you company, your I.Q. will be in serious danger."

"You do realize you just insulted not only my boyfriend but my flesh and blood?" I pulled a glass from the cabinet and poured my wine, watching as condensation immediately formed. Damn, I'd have to turn the air conditioning on soon. I always tried to hold off as long as possible, but North Carolina in April could get down-right hot at times. I took a sip and sighed.

"Yup," she responded unapologetically.

"Not all athletes are dumb, you know. You're propagating an unfair stereotype."

"Last time I hung out with those two they had a thirty-minute discussion about why people from Belgium should be called Wafflers." I really had no response to that. "And the time before that, they outlined their plan to solve world hunger by opening McDonald's franchises in impoverished nations."

I sipped my wine until I came up with a response, finally settling on, "They have other good qualities!" She laughed and we both let it go, knowing it was all in good fun. "I can't wait to see you next weekend. I miss you like crazy, girl."

Haley sighed dramatically. "I know. Me too. But, yay! You're coming to see me and we're gonna have a blast!"

"Yes! And we're going to the beach—I don't care if the water is cold. My bikini is coming out of storage!"

"Yes, ma'am! And my very modest one-piece is coming out as well." She laughed.

After we hung up, I searched the pantry for snacks. I'd eaten my weight in hot dogs, soft pretzels, and popcorn at the stadium, of course, but I was feeling peckish anyway. I tended to eat when I was troubled, but I didn't want to examine that feeling too closely, instead chalking it up to missing my best friend. I spotted a box of Thin Mints and decided they would round out my day of gluttony perfectly.

Haley and I had shared a rental house until she moved to Wilmington a couple months ago. I wasn't quite ready to take the plunge and buy a place, so I was renting an apartment on the west side until I figured out my game plan.

Truthfully, as long as the place had a decent-sized bathtub and allowed big dogs, I was good, so I didn't know what was taking me so long to commit. As if reading my thoughts, Tambo came lumbering into the kitchen, a trail of drool following him. I'd learned over time that a big dog came with big drool, and you can't get much bigger than a Great Dane. Tambo, like a lot of big burly guys I could name, was a big baby.

I took both his charcoal ears in my hands and stroked downward. "How are you, my big lug?" *Yes, I baby talk my dog. I'm not a monster.* "Were you a good boy today? Of course you were." Okay, sometimes I can even annoy myself.

"Time for a snack, Bo." That perked his ears up. In general, my dog maintained a pathetic dopey face, but when food was mentioned, his ears and eyebrows went on high alert. "Let's eat and clean up. Troy's coming over tonight."

Tambo groaned. The dog actually groaned—like seeing Troy was a big drag in his glamorous doggy life.

"What? You love it when Troy comes over." Well, maybe that wasn't technically true. Troy is not really a big dog person. He says it's the drool that skeeves him out, but I don't get what the big deal is. You just wipe it up and move on. And, besides, it's Tambo's way of showing affection—the more drool you have covering you, the more he likes you. Needless to say, I do a lot of laundry.

We chowed down in companionable silence while I checked my e-mail and work schedule for the week. I had a new message from the owner of a local horse farm I did a lot of work with. I clicked it open and read it over. One of their horses had sustained an injury this week and he wasn't recovering as well as they'd hoped. I quickly typed out a response letting the owner know I'd be happy to come over the next day, even though I didn't usually work on Sundays. The thought of the gelding in pain didn't settle well when I knew I could help out. Her response was immediate, and we made plans for the following afternoon.

I couldn't help my smile as I looked over at my dog. He'd fallen asleep right next to his bowl, his tongue hanging halfway out. How adorable was that?

The sound of the front door closing had my head automatically swinging in that direction, and Troy rounded the corner moments later. He looked hot, and his cocky grin told me I'd broadcasted my thoughts loud and clear.

"Hey, babe." His voice was husky and went directly to my girl parts.

"Hey, handsome." I got up and sashayed my way over to him, gripping his t-shirt in my hands as soon as I got close enough. "Did you get dinner?" I knew the team usually ate together at the stadium after night games.

He nodded. "Some of the guys and I hit Blue Denim for a bite."

Now that I was close and all up in his business, I probably could have guessed something like that. Gone was the freshly showered scent from earlier. In its place was the pungent odor of seafood and beer. Not that I didn't appreciate both delicacies, but I preferred them on a plate, not on my man.

Then his words hit me. I tried not to let my surprise show. Contrary to what most people think, minor league players make crap money. As in, they'd double their salary if they learned to say, "You want fries with that?" It wasn't a job for the faint of heart, but there are worse things people put up with to chase their dreams.

I'd gotten used to treating Troy and Joey to meals out whenever I could, and I was happy to do it. It wasn't like them to blow their meager paycheck on a nice seafood dinner and craft beer. Oh well, maybe they'd been scrimping for a night out. Who knows?

I caught another whiff of Troy's shirt. "I have a great idea."

His eyebrows rose as he began to walk me backward to the kitchen counter.

"I need to shower the ballpark off me. Why don't you come scrub my… back?"

Troy didn't need to be asked twice. I was quickly turned in the direction of my bedroom, his hands removing my shirt along the way.

Chapter Three

IF WISHES WERE HORSES

RETT

"No fuckin' way," I murmured to myself as I took in the number on the incoming call. Gavin eyed me curiously from his spot on the couch. I ignored him and tapped my phone's screen before the call could go to voicemail.

"Hello?" Smooth, as always.

"Brett?"

"Yeah." Sparkling phone conversation is not my strong point.

"Hey, it's Liv. From the game yesterday?" She was beginning to sound uncertain and I felt like an asshole.

I stood from the recliner and walked quickly to the kitchen. "Hi, Liv. How's it going?" That was better.

Her voice relaxed again. "Great. I hope it's okay I'm calling."

"No! I mean, it's totally fine," I answered way too quickly.

"I'm glad you called." We'd exchanged numbers outside the stadium, but I never thought she'd actually call.

"Yeah. I had fun yesterday. And, thanks to you, I now know some Spanish."

"Señora Berkovich would be proud. I'm sure it was her dream to have her students talk about balls." She giggled and it made me ridiculously fucking happy.

"Did you call for more Spanish lessons, 'cuz I might have to start charging."

"Only partly. While it's my life's goal to learn to curse in Spanish, I also had another reason for interrupting your Sunday."

"Oh? What's that?"

"How do you feel about horses?"

"Wait a second." My mouth dropped open, drawing Liv's attention to my face. She quirked a brow and I continued my thought. "You're going to stick that." I gestured to the long needle she held in her gloved hand. "Into that?" My gaze swept along the giant expanse of the enormous horse beside her.

Liv grinned and nodded to her tray of tools. "Actually, I'm going to stick *all* of these into that." She gestured to the beast with her chin. I involuntarily took a step back, causing Liv to bark out a laugh. The woman standing next to her joined in, chuckling at my expression.

"You just wait and see. Dr. Sun works wonders," the woman who'd been introduced as Pam Sutton, owner of the Red Maple Horse Farm, informed me.

Yeah. So, not only was Liv fucking adorable, fun, and sexy. She was also a damn doctor. Specifically, a veterinarian who, I'd just discovered, specialized in veterinary acupuncture. I didn't even know that shit existed before five minutes earlier.

I couldn't imagine what kind of insanity it took to poke needles into a horse ten times bigger than you, but I was about to witness it. This girl had giant... ovaries.

I watched in amazement as Liv carefully lined up the first thin needle and expertly tapped it into the flank of the horse with the tip of her finger. The horse remained completely unfazed and I stared, no longer even noticing the unfamiliar mix of sweet and sour scents or the flies buzzing around us in the barn. A second needle quickly followed as Liv made her way around various spots on the horse's leg and back. I noted the soothing touches of reassurance to the animal and the quiet voice she used to keep it calm. Before I knew it, I'd moved closer to take in the scene, standing beside Pam.

She leaned toward me. "What did I tell you?"

I just nodded and continued to watch. Liv's hair was secured in a ponytail, keeping it out of her face and affording me an unobstructed view of her golden skin and gorgeous mouth. Damn. This girl was nothing short of remarkable.

When she'd placed her last needle, Liv worked her way to the horse's spotted head, stroking its face and whispering to it.

"What's wrong with him?" I whispered to Pam.

Her mouth turned down. "He's getting older and more prone to injury and muscle strain. One of the younger horses riled him up the other day and his extensor muscles have been bound up tight ever since. Rest and time are really all we can offer—except for the acupuncture. It's a godsend, really.

Liv came back to her equipment case and withdrew a box with control knobs and a bag of wires.

"What's she going to do with that?"

Pam nodded. "Electrodes. She'll attach them to certain needles to send electric pulses to some of the muscles."

I turned to her. "No shit? I mean, really?" I quickly corrected myself.

Pam grinned and looked back at me. "No shit."

I nodded and turned back to watch Liv work. Color me impressed. This was cool as hell.

A half hour later, all the needles were removed and the horse was rewarded with a couple carrots. Liv showed me how to feed the horse without getting a finger removed, and I offered him a carrot which he enthusiastically inhaled, leaving me with a palmful of horse slobber.

I looked at my hand and then at Liv who just shrugged her shoulders and smiled. So I wiped my hand on my jeans and petted the horse's nose like she'd done earlier. His coat was warm and dusty, and he leaned into my touch. "Amazing."

"I know, right? They're gorgeous animals, aren't they?"

I nodded in return. "I've never really been around them apart from county fairs and stuff like that. Did you grow up with horses?"

She half-laughed/half-snorted, the sound somehow not ridiculous but cute instead. "No way. The only pet we ever had growing up was a cat named Tess. She was the devil herself." She hissed and mimicked scratching my eyes out with her nails. Was it wrong that it kind of turned me on? Wait, don't answer that.

I put my hands up in mock surrender and she continued, "My parents are biochemists. They're not exactly animal people. But I always gravitated toward animals. By the time I got to high school, I finally talked my parents into riding lessons and I was a goner. Most girls fall in love with horses at age seven. It took me twice as long, but I fell just as hard. Not that I've ever had my own horse or anything—I was too busy with school and too broke to afford one on my own. But there are plenty of horse owners out there who need help getting their animals enough exercise time. And I can be pretty persistent." She gave me a big grin and I laughed. I could definitely see that about her.

"So you became a vet."

"Yup." She reached up and patted the horse on the side of his neck. "It was a long road, but I wouldn't want to do anything else."

My brows drew together. "Aren't you a bit young to be a veterinarian?"

She scoffed. "Please. Did you not hear me say my parents are biochemists? Studying was a full-time profession at our house." Then she whipped her head around to pin me with narrowed eyes. "Wait. How young do you think I am?"

I shrugged to buy myself some time. Shit. This was touchy territory. If you guess too young, you're screwed; if you guess too old, same story. Personally, I thought she looked about twenty, but I wasn't about to say that. I was adding the numbers in my head and that just wasn't a statistical possibility. "Ummm, twenty-four?"

She studied my expression, probably spotting my lie, but luckily choosing to let it slide. "Twenty-six." Her tone was suspicious.

I reached out and yanked her ponytail. "See. I was close."

She smacked my hand away and stepped back to look me over. "How old are you?"

I didn't hesitate. "Twenty-five."

She nodded, giving me zero clues to her thoughts. Before my beard had grown in, people always assumed I was much younger than my true age. I'd get carded for rated-R movies, it was so bad. But then I grew into my new look and I think I just became more comfortable in my own skin. I know I'm nothing to write home about, but I take care of my body, try to work out every day, and I like the way I look. Despite what I know some people (e.g. Troy Assface) think.

Not wanting to give Liv any more of the upper hand than she already had, I took a step back and copied the slow once over on her. She wore faded jeans, a black t-shirt with a bar logo, and a pair of shitkickers. In other words, she looked fucking perfect.

She laughed at my blatant perusal and turned to the paddock, gesturing for me to follow her across the gravel pathway. She leaned against the fence, resting her elbows on the top rail. I followed suit.

"You never told me what you do, Brett."

"You mean you can't guess?" I gestured to my face and body she'd just taken her sweet time evaluating. This earned me an elbow to the side.

"Okay, fine. I'll take a stab at it." She bit her lip and paused for a moment before raising a finger in triumph. "Aha! You're a professional assassin and you have one more job to complete before you can retire."

I sent her a doleful glance. "Very funny. I work in the marketing department for Centroe."

Her mouth dropped open in surprise. Geez, I didn't think it was that shocking. "You're kidding."

"I don't joke about contract hits. Or marketing," I deadpanned.

"My parents work for Centroe!"

"Seriously?" Although I guess it wasn't that much of a stretch. She'd said they were biochemists, and Centroe is a decent-sized pharmaceutical company. Besides, they employed close to five thousand people in the area. "Small world."

"Positively microscopic." Liv shook her head.

We both let our gazes wander to the horses grazing in the

paddock. The sun warmed my skin, and I was beginning to wish I'd worn a hat.

As if reading my thoughts, Liv raised a hand to shield her eyes from the sun. "Perfect gameday weather. Too bad there's no game today."

I looked at her in mock disgust. "Blasphemer! There's always a game. This is North Carolina in the springtime."

"Don't get your panties in a twist. I meant no Guardians game."

Oh, right. I forgot it was all about her precious Troy. So, maybe I didn't know the guy, but from the little bit I'd seen and overheard yesterday, I wasn't all that jazzed to further our acquaintance. The guy was an asshole.

What Liv was doing wasting her time with him was anyone's guess.

I just shrugged, not trusting myself to comment.

Again, it was like she could read my mind. "Troy's not that bad. He's just not all that... open-minded."

Okay, I was not born yesterday. This was where I needed to keep my trap absolutely zipped. No good could come from any reply I might make to that statement.

She bit her lip and watched the horses again. "When we first started dating..." she began but trailed off. A light breeze sent some loose strands of hair to tangle in her eyelashes, and I wanted to reach out and brush them away. "I mean, he's really fun, and he's a decent guy when you get to know him. He's just kind of a man's man." She turned to me again and met my eyes. Hers were a deep chestnut with flecks of gold scattered throughout. "You know what I mean?"

Uh, not really. But I gave a noncommittal nod anyway. Man's

man? I think she meant caveman. She could do so much better than an asshole like that.

I was a damn sight better choice, if she was looking for suggestions. I mean, I may not be able to compete physically with the dude, but when it came to wit, maturity, and... uh... not dragging one's knuckles on the ground, I had that guy beat for sure.

"Okay, enough about Troy. How about we switch topics to food." Her mouth widened into a wicked grin.

That got my attention. "I'm listening." As if on cue, my stomach rumbled loudly, making us both widen our eyes.

"Something tells me you're going to like my next idea."

I was pretty sure I'd like any damn idea Liv Sun could conjure up.

"Liv. Jesus."

My cock ached in the best of ways as I moaned out her name. I couldn't help it. The image of her lips enveloping my rock-hard dick made my control slip. Unfortunately, the image was purely a product of my imagination. My very active and very filthy imagination.

I stroked myself, applying pressure to all the right spots in a well-practiced series of maneuvers. What can I say? I'm a guy. This is what we do when we're not dating or sleeping with someone. Okay, so we do it then too. We're essentially animals, I know.

My eyes squeezed shut and my head tilted back as I felt the familiar tingle rush down to the base of my spine. I could hear her sexy little moans as her lips, tongue, and hands worked my cock and caressed my balls. Her eyes gazed up at me as she took me to the back of her throat, and I was done. I blew my load and continued to stroke myself until the last spasm ran through my body and I groaned in satisfaction. Satisfaction that only lasted a few seconds.

My goddamn hand was no substitution for Liv. The girl had me twisted up with wanting her, and there wasn't a fucking thing I could do about it. I'm not a cheater and I don't like people who are. And I highly doubted Liv was the cheating type—which was a good thing. Kind of.

Shit.

The best I could hope for was that she'd eventually lose interest in Troy the Dumbass and decide she liked me instead. I could be patient when the end result was worth it.

And she was more than worth it. I just knew it.

Chapter Four

WHY YOU SHOULD ALWAYS CARRY A TAPE MEASURE

IV

I poked my tongue out to catch the drop of gravy traveling down my chin. Brett halted mid-chew and stared.

Good God.

I wanted to laugh at how transparent guys can be. One glimpse of your tongue and they're imagining other things you could do with it. Not that I wanted to encourage such thoughts from my new friend. Friend. That was it. Troy's jealousy was starting to mess with my head.

I grabbed my napkin and wiped up the remaining gravy, hopefully averting any potential awkwardness. Brett went back to chewing and I grinned.

It was Thursday, and we'd decided to meet up for lunch at Smith Street Diner before I headed over to the Guardians' stadium to catch one more game before heading to Wilmington for the weekend. Troy and Joey would be going out on the road before I got back so it was my last chance to see them play for a couple weeks.

The team traveled constantly and stayed plenty busy when they were in town too. So, that meant Troy and I hadn't had a whole lot of one-on-one time, even though he was on a local team. The off-season had been great with the guys working regular hours, but then came spring training and now the season. And, while the baseball season was all of our favorite time of year, it would be a special treat when the team had a couple home series in a row like these last ones. Troy and I had been able to get in some much-needed quality time over the last few days.

Okay, so Xbox, drinking, and sex didn't all qualify as quality time, but one out of three ain't bad. I never should have let Joey bring that damn Xbox to my place. He knows I can't say no when the gauntlet is thrown.

But the week had been fun, and I was sorry to see my two guys hit the road.

This was true, for the most part. Don't get me wrong—I love spending time with the guys. But a girl needs a little room to breathe around all that testosterone. Even though Joey and Troy shared an apartment with some other players for the season, they preferred hanging out at my place, so after a week it started to get that stale jock smell. And, truthfully, if I'd been forced to endure one more "epic" pizza belch, I would have thrown myself in front of a bus.

Not wanting to be an eternal "grass is always greener" bitch, I focused instead on my lunch partner. Brett wore a blue button-down that perfectly matched his eyes, and a pair of charcoal pants. This was finished off with well-worn chukka boots that I wished I could steal. His shirtsleeves were rolled up, exposing one of the tattoos I'd spotted the day we met.

I reached a hand across the table and tapped the inked skin. "Tell me about this."

Brett held up a finger as he finished chewing and then wiped his mouth with a napkin.

Thank you! Nobody had to teach this guy not to show off his half-masticated meal.

When he finally spoke, I choked on my drink.

"I got it at a brothel in Thailand."

I thumped my chest and threw my napkin at him.

"Okay, fine. I got wasted with my friend Gavin and somehow managed to convince the tattoo artist I was sober enough to get inked. It bled like a bitch and the guy made me come back to get it finished."

I rolled my eyes at the idiot. "Why did you choose this design?" It was a colorful rendering of a lion and it reminded me of C.S. Lewis. Maybe there was a connection.

"Honestly?"

I nodded, taking a sip of my soda.

"I have not one fucking clue. I was wasted." He shook his head and smiled. He had a great smile—straight white teeth with one side of his mouth always going higher than the other. And then there was the beard.

I snickered at his expense. "Why didn't you change it to something else when you went back? He couldn't have gotten that far on the first night."

"I had almost the whole damn outline! What was I supposed to do?"

I tsked him before responding, "Well, at least it's pretty."

Brett's eyes narrowed at me. "Don't *ever* call a guy's tattoo pretty. What is wrong with you, woman?"

I giggled and his smile was back.

"What the hell is this?"

My head snapped to the side to find Joey and Troy standing by our table. Shit. I hadn't exactly told Troy I was going to lunch with Brett.

You see, when I'd come home from treating the gelding at Red Maple the other day, Troy had been waiting for me at my apartment. He was already in a crappy mood from something that had happened at practice, and he was not pleased. We fought and he threw around some more disparaging remarks about Brett and I'd told him to shove it. We eventually made up and had some pretty stellar make-up sex, but I'd come away from the whole thing with the feeling that I'd best keep my friendship with Brett on the downlow for the time being. Unless Troy asked, I wasn't going to volunteer information about time I chose to spend with my new friend. Besides, Troy had nothing to worry about. Brett and I were just friends. Like I said.

Regardless of any decisions I had come to, it appeared Troy was forming his own opinions about the situation. I had to admit, it didn't look very good. By the puce shade of Troy's face, I surmised that perhaps I'd miscalculated. Hmm.

Plastering a smile to my face, I greeted the guys. "Hey guys! What are you doing here? Aren't you supposed to be at the stadium?"

Joey rubbed the back of his neck and glanced between me and Troy. "Um, have you taken a look outside?"

I peered around them and the other occupants of the busy diner and noted for the first time since I'd sat down across from Brett that is was raining buckets outside. How had I not noticed that?

"Oh," was all I could say. Determined to rally, I gestured to the unoccupied seats at our table. "Join us." My smile was so hard I could have cut glass with it.

Troy crossed his arms and glared at Brett, refusing to look my way. "No thanks. We're getting take-out for some of the guys before our team meeting."

I glanced at Brett, noting his own refusal to break eye contact with Troy. Why did they have to do this? I had a measuring tape in my car—I'd be happy to go fetch it so they could settle things once and for all.

I heard Troy's name being called and, without another word, he turned and headed for the counter to retrieve the bags of take-out. Joey shot me a sympathetic look and spared an uneasy smile for Brett. "Good to see you, man."

Brett lifted his chin in return. "You too."

Joey turned to follow my moody boyfriend and I called after him, "Can you please talk some sense into him?" He threw a peace sign over his shoulder. Maybe Joey could make a dent in Troy's hard head.

Appetite completely gone, I pushed my plate aside and propped my chin up with my hand. Brett, clearly not feeling a similar affliction, picked his sandwich back up and took a huge bite. He chewed slowly, his eyes never leaving my face. I couldn't for the life of me discern his expression.

"What?" I finally asked when he'd swallowed.

He took his time before responding. "I haven't checked lately, but I'm thinking your name is probably listed in the top five causes of violent crime. Either that or mental illness. I can't decide."

My gasp of indignation was drowned out by the sound of the restaurant door slamming shut.

Sounds of gunfire echoed in the hall as I entered my apartment a couple hours later. Since I'd freed my afternoon for the game, it was a major bummer to just come home, but I knew I needed to clear the air with Troy. Besides, it was my last chance to spend time with him for a couple weeks. And if the sounds of enemy soldiers being hacked to pieces was any indication, he was on my couch stewing. The fact that Tambo was nowhere to be seen was also a fair indicator that Troy was around.

Before rounding the corner, I took a deep breath and let it out, reminding myself to stay calm and try to be fair.

"Fuck! Take him out before he kills me, you asshole!" My boyfriend wore a headset and was trading curses with lord knows who. Don't get me wrong, I enjoy video games, but the thought of spending hour after hour in a simulated bloodbath is really not my idea of a good time. Give me some *Forza Horizon* and I'll race you until I get carpal tunnel syndrome. I stood and watched for another minute, figuring Troy would notice me, then finally had to step in front of the TV.

Troy scowled and never even looked at my face before gesturing for me to get out of the way. This conversation was not going to go well. Call it a hunch.

I went in search of Tambo and found him cowering under my bedspread. "Hey there, Bo." I patted his back and dropped a kiss on his head. "Did all the yelling get to you? Wanna go outside?" His ears perked and I turned to head back out, my dog at my heels. We avoided the grumpy soldier on our way and were soon headed down the stairs from my apartment, Tambo secure in his harness and me with my umbrella at the ready.

It wasn't really like Troy to be so jealous and possessive. I'd hung out with lots of ball players in the time we'd been dating, so I wondered what made Brett such a thorn in his side. This whole He-

Man thing was downright unattractive and was making it harder to remember why we'd started dating in the first place.

I mean, Troy and I had had physical chemistry from the get-go, and then there was our mutual love of baseball and our naturally competitive spirits. But he'd been charming and considerate in those first months, always with a compliment and a smile just for me. Being apart for spring training had been tough, and the new season meant we had less time together. Maybe this was how relationships went, though. I hadn't been in enough to know one way or the other, but I'd heard other people talk about working through rough patches, so that's what this probably was. Or maybe he was just stressed with the new season and hadn't found his stride yet.

I stepped out onto the walkway, but as soon as my wimp of a dog felt the first drop of rain, he backed his giant butt up and refused to follow me out. "Oh, come on, you big baby. It's just a little rain."

He continued to pull back on his lead, the fact that he outweighed me not helping my cause one bit. "You're not going to melt, and I know you have to go." God, if my clients could see me now. Some animal whisperer I was. I finally let go of the leash and walked outside, leaving Tambo at the foot of the stairs. It only took him another minute before curiosity—or a full bladder—got the better of him and he followed me out to quickly do his business before booking his booty right back to my apartment door.

This time, I was greeted with silence, the battle seemingly over for the time being. Bo wandered into the kitchen and I headed back to find Troy. He sat on the couch, wearing his typical uniform of gym shorts and a sweat-wicking t-shirt as he typed something into his phone. I approached him and mentally prepared for a fight.

"Are we okay?"

He didn't look up from his phone. "What do *you* think?"

I tried not to sigh. "You seemed more than a little pissed off at the diner."

"You caught that, did you?" Still not looking at me.

I finally sat next to him on the couch and covered his phone with my hand. "Can you please look at me while you're practicing your sarcasm?"

What I got was a glare. At least I had his attention, though.

"What do you want me to say? You think I should be totally cool with you hanging out with that Brian loser?"

I wanted to growl. "His name is Brett. And he's not a loser. Besides, he's just a friend. Since when am I not allowed to have friends?"

Troy choked out a humorless laugh. "Since this friend has a dick."

That sent my head back. "Why should that matter—especially since you keep asserting that he's a loser? I wouldn't think you'd find him threatening."

"Ha! I'm not threatened by that little twat."

I raised my brows, knowing I was probably poking a bear.

The bear growled. "He totally wants to nail you, Liv! Are you blind?" He rolled his shoulders.

I tried to brush that off, but I wasn't entirely certain it wasn't a bit of a possibility. But, dammit, I was entitled to have a friend!

Troy ran a hand over his short hair. "Let me ask you this. How would you feel if I started hanging out with some chick and going out to lunch and shit?"

My lips twisted. Huh. I hadn't really thought about it that way. I mean, we'd always been exclusive and it hadn't occurred to me to question that. I opened my mouth to respond but closed it again.

"Yeah, that's what I thought." Troy went back to typing on his phone.

I bit my lip and considered the idea some more. I'd never cheat on Troy, so I hadn't thought having a guy friend was a big deal at all. Did he think I'd cheat on him? And why did the thought of him hanging out with another woman rub me so wrong? I was a little afraid of what that said about the trust level in our relationship.

"I'd never cheat on you, Troy. You have to know that." This time I pulled the phone from his hands and he let me.

He looked at me, his eyes roaming my face as if looking for some sign of my sincerity.

I pressed on. "And if you told me you were hanging out with a woman—purely platonically—I would trust you." That might have been a lie. Oops. I *hoped* I would trust him, but I wasn't a hundred percent sure. More like eighty-five. Okay, more like fifty-five. Shit.

His eyes narrowed, gauging my veracity again, and I forced my expression to still. He shifted his mouth to the side. "Okay, well maybe I'll make a new friend, then."

I forced my lips into a smile. "Great."

"Great," he echoed.

"Well, I'm glad we got that settled." It was the only thing I could think to say. But it felt like we'd just complicated the situation a fuck of a lot further. "How about this? I promise to let you know ahead of time when I plan to hang out with Brett—or any other guy friend—and you do the same."

He didn't look all that happy, but he didn't protest either. And, honestly, I was going away in the morning and he was leaving for the road in a few days, so I didn't want us to part ways in the middle of a fight.

"Deal," he said. Then he put an arm around me. "Wanna play *Call of Duty*?"

Oh, the things I do for love... well, for *like*, in any case.

Chapter Five

MESSENGERS ARE GROSSLY UNDERPAID

RETT

"I can't believe you talked me into this!" I practically had to yell to be heard over the pounding music and shouts of the crowd.

My friend Jake turned and yelled back. "I promised Bailey a good crowd for her birthday. I wasn't about to let you stay home!"

My gaze went to the club's crowded dance floor where red and purple lights skittered across the girls assembled at its edge. Jake's wife, Bailey, was in the middle, looking a bit out of her element, and maybe a little drunk. I shook my head. The club had clearly not been her idea. My guess, she would have chosen the patio of a corner pub over the techno dance vibe and flashy short skirts surrounding her on the floor. She was decidedly un-girlie in that way. Which, of course, led my mind right where I'd been avoiding it going all day. Liv. There was another woman who forged her own path and evaded convention. The memory of her repeatedly insulting the umpire brought a grin to my lips.

But I couldn't really complain. It was nice to hang out with friends, even if it had to be at a club. Gavin had gone to the bar to grab us another round, and Emerson was out on the floor with Bailey and a handful of other girls I know—mostly the girlfriends of my buddies.

"I'm guessing she'll last another ten minutes before telling the girls to fuck off and asking to leave!" Jake shouted back. He and Bailey had a baby girl at home and didn't go out nearly as much as the rest of us.

I ran a hand over my beard and wished for air conditioning. "I volunteer to go with her!"

That got me a glare, so I was glad to see Gavin approaching with the beers. Note to self: don't joke about taking big dudes' women home.

"Hey!" yelled Gavin, handing me my beer. "Some of the Guardians players are over at the back of the club! Maybe your new friend is there!" He smirked at me, the bastard.

Of course, I'd told Gavin all about Liv and her asshole boyfriend. Like any good friend, he'd commiserated over the classic conundrum I found myself in. "She's out of town." God, my throat was going to be sore from all the shouting.

"I meant the asshole," Gavin responded.

Oh, yeah. If I had to guess, Troy was probably over there. He struck me as the type of guy who wouldn't worry too much about drinking the night before a game.

We stood there watching the women dance for a bit, not bothering to try talking over the noise. Gavin's sister, while pretty hot, was an appallingly bad dancer. And that was saying a lot coming from me. At least Gavin had the good grace to cover his eyes in embarrassment as she executed some kind of tribal mating dance with a scowling Bailey.

I signaled to Gavin and Jake that I was going to hit the head and wound my way through the sweaty crowd as best I could until I found the restrooms. The noise in there was only slightly more subdued, and like any sane guy, I left as quickly as possible. On my way back to my friends, I spotted the group of players Gavin mentioned. And, as predicted, right in the center was Troy Horner. I saw him clear as day, but he most definitely did not see me. How could he when he was busy feeling up the brunette in a short silver dress? His eyes were otherwise occupied.

Well, shit.

"Wait. So, are you sure it was him?"

I raised a brow at Bailey and wondered if they all thought I was that stupid.

Her hands moved up in a defensive position. "Sorry. Geez."

I took another swig of my beer and faced the five women at the table with me. From an outsider's perspective, I likely appear to be the luckiest man at McCoul's tonight. But it was the furthest thing from the truth.

After I'd spotted Troy Assface with his hands traveling their way to a bit of strange, I was rooted to the ground. Not that I didn't believe the guy was capable of such assholish behavior, but more shocked that he'd do it out in the wide open like that. A quick look around showed no sign of Joey, so I guess that was good. I'd hate to think Liv's cousin would be hiding something this big from her. Although, who knew? Joey could very well know all about it and be as big an asshole as his teammate. What did I know?

Troy's hand emerged from the hemline of the girl's dress and he used it to grip her hair before pulling her in for a tongue bath. Oh, for fuck's sake.

I'd seen all I could take, so I forced my feet to take me back to my friends where I promptly told the guys I was taking off. It seemed I offered just the opportunity the guys (and Bailey) had been looking for, so we all headed to the street. Once we were outside in the blessedly cooler air, I quietly told Gavin what I'd seen, which ended up being a huge error in judgment because he promptly told Emerson who told every fucking girl in our party.

Thus, I found myself occupying a table with five nosy women on the patio of an Irish pub instead of talking baseball with the guys or just going home and crashing. Jesus.

"Why do smart women always let themselves get caught up with giant douchebags?" That came from Laney, Gavin's sister.

I wanted to know the answer to that one too. Although, in my experience, smart *guys* also tended to tangle themselves with cheaters and bitches. I had a list to prove it.

"I have to assume karma takes notes. At least I hope so," said another of our crew, a tiny blonde named Fiona.

"I guess the big question is are you going to tell her?" Emerson, ever the practical one, asked the important part.

I shook my head. "I have no fucking clue." I was in uncharted territory here.

"Well, if I were you, I'd go back and punch that asshole in the nuts," Bailey advised, making me frightened, not for the first time, for her baby girl. I was thinking it would be Bailey wielding the shotgun when little Dani approached dating age.

Emerson shook her head. "Way too reactionary. Brett needs to be the bigger person here. Getting into a fight would just reduce him to Neanderthal level like the jerk of a boyfriend."

I wasn't about to volunteer my absolute certainty that I'd be hospitalized if I so much as laid a hand on Holder.

Emerson's best friend, Ari, flipped her hair back. "You need to tread carefully, that's for sure. If you want in this girl's pants, you do not want to be the messenger. They usually end up shot dead in a corner. Just sayin'."

"Who says I want in her pants? We're just friends," I protested, maybe a bit too loudly.

The women all looked at one another and were silent for beat before busting out laughing—complete with table slapping and tear wiping, like I was the funniest damn thing they'd ever laid eyes on in their lives.

Christ almighty.

My eyes shot to the guys a couple tables over, but the ones who were nice enough to meet my eyes just shook their heads in pity and went back to drinking. Assholes.

After my night out with the coven of cackling witches, I determined that there was no way I could tell Liv about Troy. But I didn't like the idea of her being betrayed, so I had to come up with an alternate plan.

To my surprise, it was Liv herself who delivered the perfect solution right to me.

Liv: *Hey! You having a good weekend?*

Me: *Sure. How about you? How's your friend?*

Liv: *Great! Except she won't let me swim in the ocean.*

Me: I'm guessing it's freezing as hell.

Liv: You guys are both pussies.

Me: Please, don't hold back, Liv.

Liv: Haha! Hey, can I ask you for a favor?

Me: Sure. But first you have to take back the pussy comment.

Liv: Fine. You're a big macho man with giant balls. Is that better?

Me: Much. Now, what do you need?

Liv: Joey forgot to leave my key for the dog sitter. He's stuck at the stadium and the bus is leaving in a couple hours. Is there any way you could run over and meet him to pick it up? I know it's a lot to ask ...

Me: I'm sure I can do that.

Liv: You're a life saver! Poor dog is probably about to pee in my bed!

She gave me Joey's number and I promised to call him to make arrangements.

Little did Liv know, I also planned to find out if Joey knew about the cheating. You can't kill your own cousin like you can some random dude you met at the ballpark. And, besides, it was better coming from someone close to her.

A couple hours later, I waited outside the stadium gates for Liv's cousin. Joey's eyes swept the sidewalk before coming to rest on me. He raised a chin in greeting and headed my way.

"Hey, man," he greeted, holding out a hand to shake. "Thanks so much for meeting me. Liv is nuts about that dog and I was going to be in deep shit."

"No problem. Where are you guys headed?" I shook his hand and then shoved both of mine in the front pockets of my jeans.

"Richmond. Not too bad. We expect to give 'em hell." He grinned, and I saw the slightest resemblance to Liv. She'd told me

Joey's mom was Chinese and his dad was French Canadian. That, as well as the distance of their relation to one another made it no surprise that I hadn't seen a family resemblance before.

I felt my palms begin to sweat as I launched into the next part of our conversation.

"I saw some of your teammates out at Fever last night."

He shook his head. "Idiots. I wanted to kick their asses. Thankfully, none of the coaching staff got wind." Then he cocked an eyebrow. "I didn't peg you for a dance-club kind of guy. No offense," he hurried to add.

I laughed. "Believe me, no offense taken. I am absolutely *not* a dance-club kind of guy. I was forced against my will."

Joey nodded. "Ah, a chick made you go."

I laughed again. "Not the way you're thinking, but yeah." Now was my chance. "So, I saw Troy."

Joey rolled his eyes, and then I watched as the general annoyance faded from his face and his expression flattened. He tilted his head and studied me. I remained silent but didn't break eye contact. God, this sucked. The moment dragged on for what felt like fucking forever when Joey finally looked to the ground and muttered a few curses.

The fact that I didn't even need to explain myself told me everything I needed to know. But I wasn't leaving until I knew what Joey's intentions were.

He put his hands to his hips and let out a breath before squinting up to the sun. "Well, looks like I've got some ass to kick."

And those were the exact words I needed to hear.

"Looks like it." We stood for another moment before he handed me the key and ran both hands through his hair in frustration—and probably a good amount of anger. "I figured she'd take it better coming from you, but let me know if there's anything I can do." I decided to leave him to his thoughts and headed back toward my car, giving his arm a hearty pat on my way.

All I could do now was wait. And hope Liv's heart wouldn't break too badly.

Chapter Six

CRUSH

IV

It was Sunday evening, and I was dreading having to leave Haley and go back home. We'd had the best weekend, and it reminded me of how much fun we used to have living together, both in Virginia where we'd gone to vet school and afterward in Greensboro. I had half a mind to pack my bags and move on over to Wilmington. But I'd worked hard to build my client base where I was, so it wasn't a real option. I just had to work harder to make more friends in my own town. I'd lost touch with all my high school friends when I left for college and veterinary school, and working on my own didn't offer much opportunity to develop new relationships. But it was time to put myself out there and meet people besides ball players.

Like Brett. I'd felt bad asking him for such a big favor, but he genuinely sounded happy to help. It was nice to have someone at my back when I was in a bind. Even if it served to further highlight my lack of friends.

He'd texted that the key was safely deposited under my doormat and my bed was, hopefully, unsullied. I hadn't asked him to go in and check on Tambo, knowing my big guy could be intimidating if you weren't used to dogs. I knew the high school neighbor kid who was dog-sitting would take care of Bo. It occurred to me that I probably should have felt uneasy sending a guy I just met to my apartment with a key, but I didn't feel weird about it at all. Either I was a great judge of character or a complete moron. Time would tell.

"Okay, how do I look?" Haley spun around and looked at me over her shoulder, gauging my reaction to her ass in the dress she'd just put on. Her strawberry blond hair was brushed to a perfect shine and she had a touch of pink in her cheeks.

"Damn, girl! I wish I had your curves." She had a great ass, despite her reservations about it, and that dress was going to knock Professor Nerdboy on his own ass.

As planned, we'd orchestrated an "accidental" run-in with Haley's neighbor the day before. I admit, it was a little over the top, but you gotta go big or go home, right? We watched him take off for a run, like the good little stalkers we were, and then proceeded to place ourselves outside the building a half hour later. Looking cute as fuck, of course, and toting along Haley's equally cute dog, Tank. When our unwitting victim returned—all toned and flushed, I might add—we pretended to have locked ourselves out.

Ted, a.k.a. Professor Nerdboy, graciously offered to let us hang out in his apartment until our fictitious friend arrived with a spare key.

Haley had been right. Ted didn't speak more than a handful of words to her or look her in the eye at all. But that didn't mean he wasn't getting an eyeful when Haley's back was turned. Ted had it bad. Turned out the guy was shy and likely lovestruck with my bestie. As well he should be. It was all I could do not to either laugh my ass off at the two of them awkwardly lusting after each other or arrange an intervention.

Luckily, Ted and Haley finally managed a somewhat normal conversation, and went so far as to make plans to go out in public together—even if it was only some function for his work. Haley had been beaming like the freaking sun ever since. And the guy *was* really cute—she had not been lying. He had black-framed glasses, killer cheekbones, and a slow inviting smile.

"Are you sure?" Haley asked, worrying her lip.

"Hey! You're gonna ruin your lipstick. Let Ted do that for you."

We both giggled like teenagers. "Promise you'll call me when you get home… or in the morning if that's where the evening takes you."

She tsked me. "I'm not even sure if it's a real date, Liv. And, besides, you know I don't give it up on night one."

I put my hands up. "This is a no-judgment zone. You do you. But I have a three-hour drive ahead of me and I'm going to need some dirt before I crash tonight."

"I wish you didn't have to go." Haley walked over in her strappy wedges and enveloped me in a hug. The top of my head reached her chin. Damn genetics! Damn Converse!

"Me either." I returned her hug. "But let's face it. There are more farm animals in my neck of the woods. They don't tend to hang out at the beach, despite what cartoons imply."

She laughed and released me. "True. But I'm sure you could

expand your client base to dolphins… or all the damn tourists crawling over this town."

I smiled. "I'll consider it as soon as your apartment complex allows dogs the size of horses. Now go have fun with your hottie neighbor!"

A knock sounded at the door, right on cue. Once again, Haley and Ted were adorably awkward with one another and it made me sigh. Loudly, it seemed, because Haley shot me a concerned look before I shooed her out the door.

Were Troy and I adorable? I mean, we had hot chemistry, that was for sure, but did we ever moon over each other? I was pretty sure the answer was no.

The week was crazy busy with work. I bagged a couple more clients, thanks to referrals from Pam and another horse farm. I also met a cow named Xanadu, which I found exceedingly humorous and prompted a call to my mother, the biggest Olivia Newton-John fan (and possibly the only one still living) on earth. Xanadu was pregnant and having problems with swelling. I did my best to fix her up before suggesting to the owner that when the calf came, perhaps Disco would be a good name. As much as I adored bovines, I didn't want one named after me—a girl had to draw the line somewhere. My mom laughed her ass off when I told her about it.

We chatted about my dad and my clients, and I promised to make it to their place for dinner soon. We also went through our usual checklist. Was I eating right? Did I carry my pepper spray when I visited new clients? Had I checked my medicine cabinet for expired medications? Had I given any more thought to her idea of writing a children's book titled *Koko and the Killer Well*? These are the topics of conversation when you're an only child and your parents are biochemist nerds.

I always changed the subject at that last one, never sure how to communicate that six-year-olds don't want to read about dead cats. Instead, I played to her interests and told her how Pam from Red Maple had given me the idea a couple months back to collect clients' expired animal medications so they could be disposed of properly (and no more Kokos had to die). This pleased my mom to no end and prompted another of her rants about people flushing drugs down the toilet and poisoning the water supply.

As a child, I'd become paranoid as a result of her stories, convinced I would grow a third arm from drinking tainted water. I told Troy that story when we'd first started dating, and he refused to drink tap water for a month. Luckily, I'd outgrown the fear and now I was channeling it into a simple thing my vet practice could do to give back to the community. And, hopefully, keep my mother from writing that terrifying book.

We talked some more about a research project she was working on at Centroe, and I even thought about asking her advice on Troy but chose not to in the end. She and I could talk about funny cows, my dad's Sinatra collection, and three-armed children, but my sex life was a bit outside both our comfort zones. We ended our call without even mentioning Troy's name.

He and I had talked on the phone a couple times, and he reminded me more of the Troy I'd first started dating. But his behavior of late refused to remove itself from my consciousness, despite any warm feelings the calls provoked.

Truthfully, though, I was lonely. Other than my clients and their owners, I spent the week by myself. By the time the next weekend rolled around, I was pretty fucking pathetic, to the point where I think, had Tambo possessed opposable thumbs, a call to the psychiatric hospital would have been placed.

On Friday night, I finally caved and sent a text to Brett. It was either that or complete my second jigsaw puzzle of the week, and nobody should ever have to sink to that level. We'd texted a couple times during the week just to say hi, and of course report about Xanadu the cow, but we hadn't made any plans or seen each other. Which was actually a good thing. Any fears I'd had that Brett was thinking of making a move were alleviated by the distance he'd taken. So, it made reaching out seem like a no-brainer and I didn't have to feel like I was doing anything Troy might need to worry about.

Me: Hey there

***Brett:** Hey. What's happening?*

I looked from my phone to the pile of puzzle pieces on my coffee table. Yeah, not going there.

Me: Nothing much. You have plans this weekend?

I grabbed the cardboard box and held it by the side of the table as I quickly swept all the loose pieces in and crammed the cover in place. I had to stop buying these damn things.

***Brett:** Just got back from a North High School game. The pitcher's sister is a friend.*

Me: Oh yeah? Is he any good?

***Brett:** Let me put it this way. I've already asked for his autograph as part of my retirement plan.*

I shoved the box under the table and leaned back on the couch.

Me: Dayum!

***Brett:** But, no. No plans yet for tomorrow.*

Me: Wanna hang out?

***Brett:** You sure Holder won't mind?*

I gave a little snarl, causing Bo's head to pop up from his spot in the corner of the living room.

Me: *He's not the boss of me.*

Brett: *Oh, I'm sorry. I thought it was past bedtime for third-graders.*

Me: *Shut up. You know what I mean. Besides, he's not back until next week.*

There was a long pause. The three dots told me he was responding, but they kept appearing and disappearing. What the hell was taking so long?

Brett: *How's Joey?*

Okay, that was a weird question. Not to mention out of left field, no pun intended.

Me: *Fine, I guess. Why?*

Another pause. I propped my feet on the coffee table as I waited. What the fuck was going on? Wait, maybe Brett had a thing for my cousin! I couldn't decide if that would make Troy feel better or worse. Then I dismissed the whole idea and decided Brett was probably just distracted.

Brett: *No reason. Anyway, as long as I get to keep all my teeth, I'm game to hang out tomorrow.*

Me: *Yay! What do you want to do?*

Brett: *I'll surprise you.*

As promised, I shot a text to Troy before I went to sleep, telling him I'd be hanging out with Brett the next day. But when I pulled the covers up to my chin and settled into my pillow, I tried not to take note of the giant grin on my face.

"You dirty, cheating liar!" I yelled.

Brett stood across the pool table, cue in hand and a sly smile on his bearded face. "I never said I wasn't good. I just said I wasn't bad."

We'd arrived at Jake's an hour earlier and grabbed a bite before moving on to the pool tables. I was no shark, but I considered myself a decent player. But Brett had just spanked my billiards ass like a disobedient sub in a flogger factory. My ego was practically black and blue.

I grabbed my beer from the high table nearby and took a sip, eying Brett over the rim. It's not that I'm a sore loser, I just want to play until I kick everyone's collective ass. *What?* There's nothing wrong with a little healthy competition.

I set my beer back down and stalked over to rack the balls up again. The crowd was light for a weekend, and the sounds of music, conversation, and clacking pool balls drifted on the air.

Brett stood across the table, spinning his cue on the top of his shoe. "I can shoot left-handed if you want. Make it a little more even."

A loud gasp escaped me before I even knew I'd made a sound and Brett practically pissed himself at the expression on my face.

"You're going down!" I jammed a finger at him, my jaw tight.

He opened his grinning mouth to respond and then snapped it shut.

I gave him a look. "What?"

"Nothing." He shook his head vehemently and scratched his cheek. "Uh, go ahead and rack 'em."

I narrowed my eyes but continued to gather the balls on the table.

"Did anyone ever tell you you're weird?"

He seemed to have recovered from his previous difficulty. "I believe you've told me that at least a dozen times so far."

I smiled and hoped it was evil. Brett walked to the other end of the table and casually took the break shot before proceeding to kick my ass once again.

Unable to stand any more humiliation, I insisted we switch things up and play darts. Brett agreed, but only on the condition I declared him to be a superior pool player. "Master of All Things Billiards," I believe was the term he used. I finally mumbled my agreement and we moved on. Another beer later, we called it quits on darts, having each won a couple rounds.

"Hmm," Brett said, stroking his beard and examining the giant Connect Four set in front of us.

My eyes traced the movement of his fingers and I had the oddest urge to reach out and run my own fingers down his beard. The coloring was slightly different from his hair, with traces of red and gold, and I wondered if it would be soft or prickly to the touch. He looked up and must have caught me staring because he shot me a quizzical look. I shook myself out of it and shrugged.

"You up for it?" He gestured to the huge game.

Before I could answer, a female voice called out Brett's name from behind us. We both turned, and a pretty woman with big boobs and a riot of red highlighted hair approached. "I thought that was you." Her smile was wide and bright as she reached her arms around Brett's neck and pulled him in for a hug.

My brows drew together and I felt something go bump in my stomach. Maybe the nachos hadn't been the best idea.

"Hi, Ginger." I couldn't see Brett's face, and his tone didn't reveal a thing. Who was this girl?

This Ginger woman pulled back, still beaming at him. "Cammie and I are hanging out on the other side of the bar. You should come join us." She had yet to look my way and I felt more than a little awkward—or maybe pissed. I wasn't sure which. For all this big-titted girl knew, Brett and I were on a date. And she had the nerve to come up and hug him and push her boobs in his face. Okay, so we weren't, in fact, on a date. And I had a boyfriend. But she didn't know that!

I cleared my throat and pasted on a smile. Brett came to attention and turned his head. "Uh, Ginger, this is Liv. A friend of mine." I put a hand out, ignoring the growing blob in my gut. God, were those nachos reproducing in there? Ginger looked me up and down and then shook my hand unenthusiastically. "Hi."

"Hi," I returned. "Brett and I were just about to play Connect Four." So we can't come play pool with your big fake boobs on the other side of the bar. Jesus, I was being a total dick.

Ginger took one more look at me and then her eyes clung to Brett as her hand stroked up and down his arm. "Well, you know where I'll be if you change your mind." Then she gave Brett a little wave and teetered on her heels back to whatever hole she'd crawled out of.

When Brett turned to me, I rose my eyebrows. But I got nothing. He just bent down to grab one of the game pieces and dropped it in a slot.

I swallowed hard, realizing for the first time that perhaps I may have formed the teensiest of crushes on Brett MacKinnon.

Well, shit.

Chapter Seven

IF YOU NEED ME, I'LL BE OVER HERE IN THE FRIEND ZONE

RETT

I was an asshole.

How could I spend time with Liv, acting like nothing was wrong, when I was keeping this huge secret from her? I'd purposely kept myself scarce the past week, hoping Joey had talked to her. I told myself I was giving her space to figure things out. My gut said she was the type of girl who would dump a guy on his ass for disrespecting her like Troy was. But it wasn't that easy. I was practically the pot to his kettle with the way I was letting this lie sit out there. I kept replaying Ari's words in my head, knowing the last thing I wanted was to be that dead messenger. But that was selfish as shit, I was beginning to admit to myself. Fucking Troy.

When Liv texted, I was ridiculously freaking happy to hear from her, and I'd been unable to say no when she asked me to hang out. Joey hadn't, in fact, talked to her—which I probably should have guessed, considering this was one conversation you wouldn't want to have over the phone. So I said fuck it and took Liv to Jake's.

The last thing I expected was to run into Ginger. That chick must have been drunk as fuck to think I might want to hang out with her and her friends. The last time I'd seen her, I'd been cleaning her puke out of my car after I found out she cheated on me. That was back in my doormat days. I couldn't believe I'd been so stupid.

It was obvious Liv wanted the whole story after Ginger took off, but there was no way I'd humiliate myself like that in front of her. The encounter all but killed the lighthearted mood of the evening and we left shortly after.

But I couldn't remember having so much fun with a girl in... well, ever. Until Ginger trotted over, that was. Liv and I traded barbs and stories, and she was fucking cute as hell when she got all pissed off about me kicking her ass at pool. It was all I could do not to kiss the pout off her face. She was sarcastic and hilarious, and brilliant. And she ate like a frat boy and enjoyed craft beer. In a word, she was perfect.

And she wasn't mine.

I ran a hand through my hair and tried to focus on the computer screen before me. The job didn't require much concentration, as I was just proofreading some press releases, but I had to force my mind off of Liv and my less-than-noble thoughts about her and her tight little body.

My phone dinged with a text notification, and I had the damn thing out of my pocket before I could blink. I couldn't help the disappointment when it wasn't Liv's name I saw on the screen.

Gavin: *Wanna grab a beer tonight?*

I looked back at my computer screen and then at the time. Fuck it. I wasn't getting anything done and it was almost five o'clock.

Me: *Absolutely. Don't you have training?*

Gavin was a coach at the Baseball Academy and worked most evenings.

Gavin: *Schedule got messed up so I have the night off. Where do you want to go?*

I was tempted to say Jake's, but that wouldn't help get my mind off Liv in the least.

Me: *I'll meet you at Joymongers. I'll be the one drinking away his sorrows at the bar.*

Gavin: *This is about a girl, isn't it? You must have been a giant prick in a former life.*

As my best friend, of course Gavin had been a witness to all my dating failures. It was a wonder he hadn't beaten some sense into me yet.

Me: *Later.*

"I would say you need to get laid, but that's usually the root of your problem. Not that I'm faulting your dick or anything. It's really his only job." Gavin raised his glass, apparently in a toast to my dick. How had my life degraded to this?

"Dude, can we stop talking about my junk?"

"I second that." Fiona said, setting her drink down on the table. She and her boyfriend, Mark, had decided to join us at Joymongers, a local craft brewery. Emerson was still at work, which wasn't all that unusual since she was a corporate lawyer and a successful one at that.

I stared at Fiona's drink as she settled herself on the barstool, adjusting her skirt and flipping her blond hair over her shoulder. Mark watched her every move, as usual. "What the hell are you drinking?" I had to ask, since Joymongers only serves beer and her glass contained something that was decidedly not in the beer family.

She waved me off. "Oh, one of the bartenders keeps a couple bottles of wine in the back for his girlfriend. I got him to share."

I just nodded, unsurprised at this. Fiona could charm her way out of a high-security prison, so getting a free glass of wine at a brewery was par for the course.

Mark turned to the bar, his back suddenly straight. "Which one?"

Fiona's hand stopped him before he could get up. "Oh, for God's sake. He was just being nice, you big beast. Didn't you hear the part about the girlfriend?" Mark reluctantly settled back down and sipped his beer. Mark was another one of these guys who could beat me into the ground with both hands tied behind his back. Luckily, he counted me as a friend, so we'd be on the same side if a fight broke out. Or the zombies rose.

"So, did your baseball girl break up with her assmuncher boyfriend?" Fiona sipped her wine and all eyes landed on me.

I shook my head. "No. She doesn't know about the cheating yet. But her cousin knows, so I think he's going to tell her when the team gets back in town."

"Wait. So you're dating this girl while she still has a boyfriend?" Mark asked. This made me want to laugh because word on the street said Mark used to be the biggest manwhore in town before he and Fiona hooked up. And now he was Mr. Sensitive? But I didn't laugh, of course, since I wanted to remain on his side should the zombies choose Greensboro to start their reign of terror. I'm no idiot.

"I'm not dating her. We're 'friends.'" I made the dumbass air quotes.

Both Mark and Gavin winced. "Friend-zoned. That blows."

"Yeah. Apparently every hot girl on earth thinks I'm 'nice.'" Another stupid air quote and another wince from the guys.

"That's the fucking kiss of death," Gavin said and then patted me awkwardly on the shoulder, seemingly feeling obligated to offer some kind of condolence. I drained half my beer.

"Oh, please." Fiona rolled her eyes. "Stop feeling so sorry for yourself and do something about it."

"What do you want me to do? She doesn't see me in that way!"

She shot me a look—the kind that only women are capable of executing. "Then *make* her see you! Stop being so damn polite and just grab the girl and kiss her!"

"She has a boyfriend, Fiona." I went for my own look, but it bounced right off her.

"Details. That shit will sort itself out soon enough. And if she chooses to stay with that twat sandwich, she doesn't deserve you."

I scowled at her and she just smiled.

"Yeah, that sounds like the worst plan in the universe. Get the girl to like me by making her cheat on her boyfriend—the one who's an asshole because he's cheating on her. Great plan."

"Fine. Then just wait for her to break up with the guy and use your nice-guy status to be the one to console her. Then you work your moves and get the girl. Easy." Another hair flip.

That time I did laugh. Like it would be so easy. "You're fucking crazy."

"Normally, I'd defend you from insults, Shortcake, but I'm with Brett on this one," Mark said. "It ain't easy breaking out of the friend-zone. At least, I imagine it isn't. Not that I've ever had that problem." Smug asshole.

He and Gavin both snickered and I was tempted to knock their beers into their laps. But then I'd have to spring for another round.

Fiona gave her boyfriend the stink-eye. "You poor thing. It must have been torture having women see you as nothing but a walking penis."

Mark's smile died, but Gavin just laughed louder.

"Hey!" Mark scowled at Fiona. "That's not what I meant."

She just patted his arm. "Be happy it was a dick they saw you as, and not an asshole." She smiled beatifically at him, making me momentarily second-guess my desire for a girlfriend.

Me: Hey. Haven't heard from you. You okay?

No response. It had been over a week since I'd seen or heard from Liv. I was beginning to think our friendship was over, which made my chest tighten—not that I didn't deserve it. But I also considered the possibility that she was laying low and licking her wounds after Joey told her about Troy.

When I still hadn't heard back from Liv by the next morning, I decided to text Joey directly. The image of feisty, larger-than-life Liv crying alone in her apartment made my gut hurt.

Me: Hey. It's Brett. Liv's been MIA. Did you tell her yet?

The three dots appeared and I waited, my foot tapping under my desk.

Joey: We'll be back in town in about an hour. Going to track her down during my break. If I can't find her, I'll do it after tonight's game.

Me: *Good luck.*

Joey: *I have a feeling I'll need it. Oh, and if you show up tonight, don't be surprised by the two black eyes Horner is sporting these days. I broke the fucker's nose.*

Me: *Best news I've heard all day.*

Well, at least I had one thing to smile about. I didn't want to think what it said about me that a broken nose and two black eyes made me downright jolly.

I still wore a satisfied grin when I walked to the parking lot with Vic, one of the other marketing guys, to grab some lunch. Just as I reached for my door handle, a hand jerked me back by my shoulder and I found myself face-to-face with Troy fucking Horner.

"Why can't you mind your own fucking business, you freak?!" He growled in my face and came so close I could make out the capillaries in his eyes. The same eyes circled with purplish-green skin. He still held my shirt in his fist.

"Hey, Troy. Good to see you too." Yeah, I was tempting fate, but I couldn't help it. This only caused him to jerk his fist, sending me off balance. No worries, though—he was doing a fine job of holding me upright all on his own.

"Oh, shit," I heard Vic mumble from the other side of the car— where he remained, mind you. Not that I blamed him.

"Shut your hole, smartass! This thing is between me and Liv and you need to disappear. Got it?"

I wanted to wipe my face of the spittle that had just landed on my cheek but didn't think this was the opportune moment.

But fuck it. I was done stepping back.

"Well, at least we can agree on one thing, Horner." Troy's

brows drew together and I continued, "It *is* between you and Liv." I let my voice drop. "And just between you and *me*, I'm hoping she breaks your fucking jaw." I let my eyes rest on the tape covering his nose and raised a brow at him.

Troy's lip curled and he let my shirt go. Then he put his fist in my stomach and I went down like a tree to his lumberjack.

Chapter Eight

MEN SUCK—WELL, MOSTLY

 IV

"Hey! This is a nice surprise." I got up from my desk and rounded it, only to be wrapped up in Joey's big arms. Tambo grunted his hello from the corner of my office and laid his dog head back down to resume his nap. "I saw your stats for the last couple series. Lookin' good, cuz!" He finally released me and I stepped back to lean against my desk. Joey's appearance was a happy coincidence since I was looking for a distraction. I'd already rearranged my client files in order of cuteness and called my mom to talk about nothing.

"Thanks." He put his hands in the pockets of his gym shorts and didn't quite meet my eyes under his ballcap. What the hell?

"Joey?" My eyes narrowed.

"Um, I was on break, so I just thought I'd stop by and see how you were doing."

Well, that would take a few hours to communicate, so I went for the short version, sure that this was only a stall tactic anyway. "I'm okay. How about you? You look strange."

He sent a pained smile my way. Okay, this was ending now.

I pushed off my desk. "What's wrong? You look like you're either guilty or constipated—I can't decide which. Spit it out."

Joey grimaced and then spoke in a rush of words. "Troy's been cheating on you and I broke his nose. He's a complete asshole and you deserve way better. I'm sorry." He sucked in a breath and held it, eying me carefully.

I stared at him blankly until his words registered. Troy was cheating on me.

My boyfriend was cheating on me.

I tilted my head and crossed my arms over my chest. "As in, flirting with some cleat chasers or as in, sticking his dick in them?" This wasn't the time for subtlety.

"The last one." Joey's voice was quiet as he gripped the back of his neck with one hand.

My head snapped back. Wow. I mean, holy fucking wow! A sudden image flashed in front of my eyes of Troy pounding into some girl in a slutty nurse's costume. Don't ask me why my imagination turned her into a stripper. This was my personal horror story —I could pick whatever characters I pleased. My stomach lurched a bit but I took a breath and gathered myself.

"How long has this been going on?" My voice was strangely calm.

"I'm pretty sure since spring training." He winced, as if telling me physically pained him. Ah, Joey.

I let that bit of news settle for another moment. "And how long have you known?" Strangely, the answer to this question seemed almost more important.

Joey swallowed. "I found out the morning we left for Richmond and then I asked around to get the full story."

Okay. That wasn't as bad as I'd feared.

"And how did you find out? Did you catch him... with someone?" The image made me want to puke.

He adjusted his cap and averted his eyes. "Uh, actually, your friend Brett told me. He saw Troy with some chick at Fever."

What the actual fuck? I'd just seen Brett last weekend and he hadn't said a thing! Jesus freaking Christ! Then I remembered his weird texts about Joey and the pieces started to fall into place. Dammit!

This also explained why Troy's calls and texts over the last week had been overly solicitous and completely inconsistent with his recent mood—and his recent stats. He was buttering me up, hoping I wouldn't dump his ass. He had a rude surprise waiting for him, that was for damn sure!

"Are you okay?" Joey asked, stepping closer.

I took a breath and put the Brett thing aside for the moment, concentrating on the giant mess with Troy. A niggle in my subconscious had told me more than once that if I didn't have one hundred percent trust in Troy's faithfulness, there was something seriously wrong. Why hadn't I listened?

I'd probably been distracted by his hot body and all the orgasms he handed out like candy. Right. But I wasn't the only one he was handing them out to. I felt the bile rise again and took another breath. Thank fuck we'd always used condoms.

Joey pulled me into his arms again, and a couple tears landed on his shirt. I felt... sad. Betrayed. Pissed. But, oddly, not all that heartbroken.

"Can you do something for me, Joey?"

"Anything. You name it." He squeezed me a bit tighter.

"Can you please describe in extensive detail what it felt like to break his nose?"

Joey barked out a laugh and kissed the top of my head. "Nothing would make me happier."

"I am going to kill that jerk! How dare he?!" It was possible Haley was even more pissed off than I was. Indignation thundered over the line as she continued to outline her plan to dice Troy's penis up in little pieces and feed it to wild dogs while he watched. I made a note to never piss Haley off.

"Thanks, Hales, but I wouldn't want you to go to jail. He's not worth it." I gazed out my windshield at the office building across the way.

She made a grumbling sound and I was grateful that she didn't go the route of "I never did like that guy." But I wished more than ever that we still lived together. If there were ever a time for a girl to lean on her best friend, it was during a breakup with a dirty, cheating liar. We were doing our best, though, with the miles between us.

"Livvy, I'm coming to see you as soon as I can and we're burning anything even remotely related to that rotten excuse for a man. Then, I hate to say it, we're going to get you tested."

I quietly banged my forehead against my steering wheel and heard Tambo whine from the backseat. Shit. I knew she was right, even if Troy and I had always used condoms. A full-body shudder ran through me at the thought of how many women Troy may have been with. It just made me more pissed off.

"After that, we're getting drunk," Haley promised.

Thank God for best friends.

After we hung up, I put a call in to the management office at my apartment complex asking them to change the locks on my unit. I knew it would cost me, but it was worth it. It was late afternoon and there was no way I was going home and risking a Troy encounter. He was supposed to be at the stadium until after their game tonight, but with the way he'd been blowing up my phone, I couldn't take the chance. Earlier in the afternoon I'd visited a client, only to return to my car and find eleven voicemail messages from the ass. I erased them without listening to a single one and promptly blocked his number.

I really don't know why he expected anything different. As far as I was concerned, we were done. Joey could come get his stuff from my place because I had no desire to ever lay eyes on Troy again. Which was a major bummer since he played on Joey's team. Ugh. That only made him more of an asshole!

With no other idea of where to go, I finally drove to a movie theater and bought a ticket, leaving Bo to nap in the car. Then I tried to forget everything for a couple hours as I watched dinosaurs chase Chris Pratt and ate a bucketful of popcorn. By the time the movie let out, I knew the Guardians game had started so I drove us home.

It only took me twenty minutes to pack a bag and gather Tambo's things before I was back in the driver's seat, still having no clue where to go. No hotel would take my big dog, and it wasn't as if I could go to Joey and Troy's place—this was where having some goddamn friends would really come handy. I briefly considered driving home to my parents', but they would ask too many questions, and I wasn't ready for a parental-level inquisition.

Before I could overthink it, I scrolled through my contacts and hit the call button. Brett picked up on the second ring.

"I'm kind of pissed at you right now, but can my dog and I sleep on your couch tonight?"

"Hey, big guy." Brett scratched Bo's head and that was all it took for my dog to forgive any wrongdoing the man would ever commit. Pushover.

I stood in the doorway of Brett's townhouse feeling more than a little awkward. This had not been one of my better ideas. Brett looked back to me and seemed to take an inventory of some kind before letting out a breath and attempting a smile. "You okay?"

He stepped back so I could come in. I dropped my bag on the floor and sighed. "I've been better, I gotta be honest. I hadn't anticipated being homeless, that's for sure."

Brett chuckled politely at my lame joke and picked up my bag before gesturing for me to go ahead of him. His place was cleaner than I would have guessed for a couple guys in their mid-twenties, but the décor was *all* guy. Meaning, apart from a couple framed memorabilia pieces, the walls were bare and everything was decorated in varying shades of boring.

My dog immediately began his survey of the place, as was his doggy right and duty. I turned to Brett. "I hope there's no food on the table or counters. Or, I should probably say, I hope there *wasn't* any food. Because it's long gone now."

He grinned at me. "Maybe a few crumbs, but nothing else." Then he looked at his shoes. "You want to talk about it, Liv?"

"I don't have a problem with Bo eating your crumbs." I faked a smile.

Brett sent me the same look a teenager would direct at an intolerably uncool parent.

I groaned. "You really want to do this now? I just got here. The elephant hasn't even had a chance to settle in."

"Haha. Fine. Let's have a beer instead." Brett led the way to the kitchen but stopped abruptly, causing me to plow into him. My hands jumped out to steady me and ended up resting on his back. I was surprised at the firmness and warmth that met my palms. Brett wasn't a big guy by any means, but the dude was kind of built. Who knew? Before I even realized what I was doing, my fingers trailed upward to his shoulders, causing his muscles to tense under my touch. Pulling myself out of the moment, I stepped back and felt my face begin to color.

Brett turned, and his jaw ticked. I couldn't imagine what he must be thinking. I decided the best course of action was to go on the defensive. "What did you stop for?"

His brows drew together and then he blinked a couple times. "Oh. I just remembered you were mad at me and it might not be smart to turn my back to you." He swallowed thickly and his eyes homed in on my mouth.

Was is hot in here? And why was he staring at my mouth? Damn, this was uncomfortable. Wait. I *was* mad at him—I'd almost forgotten. I tried to conjure up my angry feelings from earlier, having little success. "I thought we weren't talking about this." I pushed my way in front of him and went straight to my dog, petting him to occupy my hands.

"I'll get our beers." Brett circled around me, but the air between us felt alive. It had been such a mistake to come here!

I punched the pillow and tried to settle back in, Tambo grumbling at the disturbance to his sleep. Crap on a cracker. This was no good.

I'd given up arguing with Brett when he insisted I take his bed. His stubbornness was almost on par with mine. But I could tell his man code wouldn't let him leave me on the couch, so I gave in eventually—for Bo's sake, of course. My dog was such a diva. But there was no sleep to be had.

Brett and I had spent the evening on opposite ends of his couch pretending to watch *Westworld*. At least *I* was pretending. What in the hell was wrong with me? I'd had my heart ripped out by a complete dickhead just this morning and here I was so… *aware*… of this other guy sitting eighteen inches to my left. Yes, I calculated it. I was practically obsessed with that patch of beige separating us.

Sure, it was probably more my pride that Troy had destroyed. And my trust, of course. But still. This was not okay. And, worse yet, I couldn't seem to get a read on Brett. He gave new definition to poker face. He and Lady Gaga freaking owned the poker face.

Neither of us brought up the subject of Troy or why Brett hadn't told me about the cheating himself. I supposed I had a few guesses, but I still wanted an explanation from him.

I rolled on my back and yanked the pillow out from under my head. It was the only thing I had on hand to muffle my frustrated scream.

Chapter Nine

ANIMAL INSTINCT AND TIGHT SHORTS

RETT

There weren't enough sheep in the fucking universe to lull my horny ass to sleep. I'd spent the better part of the evening trying to hide the tent in my pants as Liv lounged beside me on the couch wearing practically no clothing. In some circles, I suppose her miniscule shorts and tank top would qualify as pajamas, but to my mind, they only served as neon signs pointing the way toward the forbidden land.

I scrubbed my hands through my hair and clenched my teeth. Rubbing one out was not an option. The walls were way too thin. I briefly considered going out to my car but then remembered I didn't ever want to be *that* guy. For once, I wished that Gav and Emerson would have chosen our place for their nightly bonkfest.

At least then I wouldn't be so worked up in the knowledge that this girl I craved was practically within arm's reach.

"Dammit." I threw the blanket off and strode to the kitchen, thinking maybe another beer would do the trick. I'd be useless at work in the morning if I didn't at least get a few hours of shuteye. I grabbed a Hoppyum and popped the top, leaning my butt against the counter. A dim ray of light penetrated from the back-porch lamp but did little to illuminate the kitchen. I ran the bottle cap between my thumb and fingers, letting the rough edge bite into my skin to distract me. It was no use. I tossed it forcefully toward the trash can and missed. Even inanimate objects were out to taunt me —a notion that was confirmed when I bent to pick the cap up and banged the back of my head on the counter on my way back up. "Shit!" I covered my head with one hand and brought the beer bottle to the counter with a thud. Immediately, a fountain of foam spilled over the top and cascaded across the surface and onto the floor. "Goddammit!"

I grabbed a roll of paper towels, but before I could even begin to clean up the mess, I was all but shoved out of the way by an enormous furry beast who proceeded to lap up my IPA from the floor, cabinets, and counters in record time.

"What the hell is going on?" This came from the girl trailing the beast. The one in the tiny pajamas and mussed hair. Good Christ.

"Nothing. Sorry!" I rubbed my head and listened to Tambo smacking his lips and tongue around, but despite my intentions, my eyes drifted directly to Liv's tank top and her stiffened nipples pushing against the fabric. My cock woke up again as if summoned by her breasts and doing his damnedest to climb as close as possible to them. I brought the roll of paper towels down to hide my erection, but all it did was draw Liv's eyes down. "I just spilled a beer. I got it."

The corners of her lips turned up. "I can see that."

It was then I realized I was wearing a t-shirt, boxer briefs, and nothing else. Fuck. Me. I snatched the beer bottle up in a panic and turned to the sink. "Uh, yeah. So, I hope it's okay that your dog just drank a beer."

"Bo!" She scolded the dog but didn't sound like she meant it. "You pledging a fraternity now?" I heard her pat him. "Go on. You cleaned it up enough."

The dog smacked his jaws one more time and his nails clicked on the tile floor as he retreated to the living room.

I glanced over my shoulder. "Sorry I woke you up."

"You didn't. I was having trouble sleeping." She sidled up to the counter next to the sink where I stood with my crotch pressed against the cabinet. "You know, unfamiliar bed," she explained, leaning forward and propping her cheek on a hand. "What about you?" I swear I caught a smirk threatening.

"Uh, same. Couldn't sleep." This was ridiculous. "You want a beer? I've got a couple more in the fridge, unless you want to finish the one your dog started."

"No, thanks." She pushed back off the counter and I turned around without thinking. Her eyes shot right to my junk and I winced inwardly. My only hope was that it was too dark for her to see much of anything.

But it was no use. She pulled her lips between her teeth to suppress her smile... or laugh... or whatever the hell she was thinking.

I threw my hands out, launching the paper towel roll over the counter and into the next room. "I'm a guy! What do you want me to say?" I brought one hand back in a vague gesture up and down her small frame. "A girl walks around in her underwear and the cock gets a mind of his own."

Her mouth flew open and she looked down at her clothes. "I'm not in my underwear!"

"May as well be," I shot back. I had nothing to lose at this point. I may as well have been standing there stark raving naked with my dick bobbing in the air.

"You're the one in your underwear!" Again, she drew attention back to my straining cock before having the decency to look back up at my face.

"I guarantee the material I'm wearing could make six of what you're wearing!"

"These are pajamas." She pulled at the material of her top, making it stretch tighter over her tits.

"You're not helping!" I shouted, which just brought her attention to my dick yet again. At this rate, it was likely to make an appearance over the waistband of my boxer briefs.

She crossed her arms. "Are you sure about that?" She raised a brow and I couldn't take it anymore. I stalked past her. It wasn't that I couldn't find humor in the situation—or, more likely, wouldn't be able to a few weeks from now. It was that I didn't want to be a joke to her, and I was afraid that's what I might be.

"I'm sorry." She grabbed my arm as I passed, and the feel of her fingers flexing on my skin stilled me. "Sometimes I can't help myself. I mean, you are standing here in your underwear with a sizable hard-on. It's not like I can just ignore it."

"I'd actually prefer if you did." Then I paused and backtracked a few seconds. She said sizeable. Nice.

"Well, you're obviously looking at *my* body. You can't expect me not to look at yours," she retorted.

And that's when I decided to hell with it. I turned and gave Liv such a thorough appraisal from toes to head that I probably could have written a dissertation on her appearance afterward.

Liv shifted on her feet and crossed her arms again, but not before I took note that her nipples were even more prominent in her top than before. Huh. Seemed like I wasn't the only affected party. I tilted my head and raised a brow, letting my eyes shift meaningfully from her breasts to her face like a complete jackass.

"Oh, for the love of God." She rolled her eyes, but if the lights had been on, I would swear she was blushing despite the eyeroll.

"I see I'm being of some help to you as well." You know, just in case I wasn't being enough of an ass.

"It's cold in here." She pursed her lips.

"It's at least 75 degrees."

She huffed, struggling to come up with a response, and chose instead to take a page from my book and stomp by me. My cock jumped in my shorts. Liv in a tank top and tiny shorts was a fucking turn-on, but Liv in a tank top, tiny shorts, and a temper was pure carnal kryptonite.

"Good night, Brett," she snapped, heading to the stairs.

"Oh, come on, Liv! It's just animal instinct. You should know all about that." I didn't try to hide my smile when she shot me a glare over her shoulder before disappearing up the stairs. Tambo trotted after her, and I lay back down on the couch and grabbed the remote, knowing it would be a while before I could sleep.

Unfortunately, the best thing on was an infomercial for an egg extractor. I never knew one needed help cracking an egg, but clearly someone did since our economy generally works on a pretty careful supply and demand process. By the time the first ten minutes had passed, I was seriously considering pulling out my credit card. I mean, who wants egg shells in their cookie dough? Not me, that's for damn sure.

"Brett." I almost didn't hear her, but the flash of white in my peripheral vision led me to Liv, standing still at the bottom of the stairs.

I sat up. "Hey. I was just watching—"

"Shut up." She cut me off and then strode toward me with purpose. What that purpose was, I couldn't be sure, so I dropped the remote and put my hands up. Liv swept them aside, grabbed my face between her hands, and landed a hard kiss on my mouth.

It was possible she split my lip, but I didn't give one shit, instead getting with the program as soon as fucking possible. The kiss was urgent, and I slanted my mouth to fit to hers, all the while my mind filling with questions. Was she doing this to prove a point? Gain back the upper hand? Was this kiss something she'd been thinking about as long as I'd been thinking about it? And, mostly, did she *mean* this kiss?

Liv gave my lower lip a small bite and I heard myself groan before I sank my hands into her hair and delved my tongue past her teeth and into her mouth. She tasted like mint and something sweet I couldn't identify, and when I inhaled, I was met with that citrusy aroma I associated with her. Her tongue ran across mine and we tasted one another as we pushed further into the kiss.

Her hands left my face and skated down across my shoulders and back as she pulled me toward her. She was straddling my lap by this point, and my hips reflexively drove upward to the heat between her legs. Those shorts were doing a shit job of preserving her modesty, and mine had been left behind an hour ago. She let out little moans when my cock pressed firmly against her and I was about ready to lose my mind.

As our lips and tongues danced, my hands explored her silken hair and continued down over her back and finally to her ass where I cupped and squeezed, drawing more sounds from Liv.

She finally tore her mouth from mine to give us a moment to breathe and I watched as her lips turned up into a grin.

Oh, hell no. I flipped her onto her back and she yelped in surprise, but I covered her mouth with mine again, silencing her. She wound her legs around me and I kissed her like I had an urgent end-of-the-world message to communicate and the only way to do it was through Liv Sun's hot, wet mouth.

When we broke apart again—oxygen being a bothersome necessity—she squeezed my ass and pressed her hips up. It was all I could do to not rut like a teen in the throes of puberty. Liv's hand drifted between us and I was thinking my night was cruising its way to a historic high. But when the back of her hand pressed against the exact spot where Horner's punch had landed, I hissed out a breath.

"What's wrong?" Liv's eyes found mine and I took in the sight of her flushed cheeks and swollen lips.

"Nothing." I went back in for another kiss, but she pushed against my chest.

"Not nothing. You flinched like I hurt you." Before I could protest, she lifted my shirt and gasped. "What the hell happened here?"

I tried brushing her hands to the side but she wasn't having it. "Nothing." Her brows shot for the ceiling. "Just guy stuff." I leaned in again. "And I'm much more interested in girl stuff right now."

Liv slipped out from under me and went for the lamp by the couch. I blinked at the brightness. We'd been doing just fine with the light from the TV. This was bound to kill the mood entirely.

She yanked my shirt up which, in any other situation, would have had me helping her right along. But there was nothing I could do.

"You've got contusions."

Ah, it seemed Dr. Sun was in the house.

"Where else are you hurt?" Her touch assumed a clinical demeanor, a glaring contrast to just moments before.

"Nowhere. I swear." I tried pushing her hands aside again but she just glared at me.

"It looks like a horse kicked you in the stomach and ribs. But I guarantee you haven't been around any horses since..." She stood up suddenly and backed away from the couch. "Oh my God. It was Troy, wasn't it?"

I thought about lying, but I'd had enough of keeping things from Liv. All it had won me was an ulcer and dirty looks. I put my hands out. "Fine. He punched me. But I swear I'm fine. It's not the first time I've been punched. If you knew me growing up you'd know this is no big deal." There was a time when I'd tried making up for my size by picking fights. Thankfully, I smartened up a bit once I hit adulthood.

Liv drove her hands through her hair and her gaze skittered around the room. "I can't believe he did that!" She shook her head. "I mean, I *can* believe it, but I'm pissed the fuck off!" She turned for the stairs and I got up to follow her. "I gotta go." Her voice was panicked. Distracted.

"Liv, you don't need to go anywhere. It's the middle of the night." And we were kind of in the middle of something.

She paused, her back still to me, and I watched her shoulders slump. "I'm so sorry, Brett. This was a mistake."

No fucking way. "What are you talking about?" I wasn't even sure if she meant her coming to stay with me or us making out, or even us being friends. In any case, it was no mistake.

"God, I can't believe I let this happen," she murmured before sprinting up the stairs.

And that gave me my answer. It was unmistakable in her tone, her words, and her retreating footsteps. Regret. She regretted letting things get physical between us. She'd just had her heart broken and I was the asshole who'd taken advantage of the situation. Instead of being her friend, I'd tried to make myself into something more. And she didn't want that.

Even if her body said differently, her heart and mind were on the opposite side. Something I had to respect and be mindful of—which was why I didn't follow Liv up the stairs and didn't say a word when she and her giant dog walked out the door five minutes later.

Chapter Ten

OLIVIA NEWTON-JOHN DID NOT PREPARE ME FOR THIS

 IV

There weren't enough derogatory names in the Urban Dictionary to call myself, but I settled on a classic. Asshole. What had I been thinking being such an asshole to Brett?

When he'd started taunting me, all reason abandoned me. I got caught up in the banter and couldn't seem to help myself. I didn't consider the consequences, instead saying *to hell with it* and basically jumping him.

And it had been so good. That boy kissed like it was an Olympic sport and he had a mantel full of gold medals. But I was being so unfair. We were friends, and there I was, ready to throw the whole thing out just because he'd challenged me and I was nursing a tiny crush.

I needed to think with my brain and not my erogenous zones or my pride. Troy physically assaulted Brett. And if I knew anything about Troy, he wasn't one to let go of a grudge. He'd be only too happy to deliver more of his caveman justice if he saw Brett again. Jesus. What must Brett have thought of me? I'd just broken up with this barbarian hours before, and there I was mounting him like a horny lion on his couch when he'd graciously offered to let me spend the night.

Brett deserved so much better than to be treated like sloppy seconds or just a body I could use to salve my wounds. God, he probably thought I was not only an asshole, but some indiscriminate hobag too. Nice, Liv.

I turned my car into the dirt forecourt of the barn and parked. Tambo grunted once from the backseat and then continued with a sigh and more doggie snoring. It was still dark, but the lamps on either side of the main barn door illuminated the expansive wood surface. After I'd hightailed it out of Brett's place, I didn't know where to go, but memories of other sleepless nights brought me back to where I felt at home.

I got out and walked to the latched door, trying my best to be quiet so I didn't wake anyone at the main house. These were the stables where I'd spent a good chunk of my high school years, not to mention any opportunity I found since then. I knew I'd be dead tired when morning came, but I needed this.

I unlatched the door and it swung open with a drawn-out creak, the sound repeating through the barn as I closed it behind me. My steps took me to the third stall on the left where a beautiful Palomino stood surrounded by darkness. The scent of hay, horse sweat, and manure conjured an easier time and I breathed it in gratefully as I reached out to press my hand to Minky's long nose. "Hey, girl," I whispered.

She blinked and sniffed a couple times before tilting her head to catch more strokes from my outstretched hand. She'd aged a bit since the last time I'd seen her a couple years ago. But she was still a gorgeous girl.

"How've you been, Minky Girl?" I ran my fingers over her smooth gold coat. I, of course, didn't expect a reply, but I thought it was polite to ask. "Personally, I'm kind of a mess, if you want to know."

She lowered her head and I took that as an affirmative.

"I just broke up with this guy. I totally should have known better than to date him in the first place. He had player written all over him." I leaned my head against the blaze on Minky's face. "And I think I took advantage of a friend of mine. I don't really know what to do about it." It was so hard to figure out my feelings for Brett in the midst of all the Troy upheaval. "He'd been a good friend, and I might have permanently ruined things."

Minky nickered, and I had a bit of trouble deciphering that one. "You think I should talk to him?" That got no reaction. "I didn't know what else to do, so I ran away. I probably should have stayed and apologized." Yeah, that would have been a less assholish move, in retrospect.

She didn't have anything else to contribute on the subject so I silently stroked her for a few minutes before settling on the dusty barn floor and leaning against her stall. We talked a bit longer, but I eventually drifted off, her steady breathing lulling me to sleep where I sat, thoughts of Brett's long fingers on my skin making me sigh into slumber.

This was a bad idea.

What if he didn't want to see me?

What if he wouldn't talk to me?

Brett stepped out from the glass doors and it was too late to run away. Despite the bright sun reflecting off every shiny surface in the lot, he spotted me in no time—which I suppose was unsurprising since I was sitting on the hood of his car. He paused for a moment but resumed his steps, his expression unreadable. It was the day after I ran out of his place, and I was dead on my feet after precious little sleep and a day filled with clients. But I couldn't leave this hanging out there. So I pasted a smile on my face and waved. He didn't wave back, but he also didn't flip me off, which I considered a promising sign.

He wore a gray button-down and black pants, and there were dark circles under his eyes which most certainly mirrored my own.

"Hey," I said when he was close enough I didn't have to shout.

"Hey, Liv." His voice was quiet and I didn't like it. He let his gaze drop to the side as he approached and halted a few feet from me, his thumb and forefinger absently running over his mustache—the same mustache that had swept over my top lip while we'd been kissing like horndogs just last night. Ugh.

"How was work?" I began lamely, gesturing to the huge brick Centroe building behind him.

He shrugged. "Just another day, I guess." He still didn't meet my eye, so I knew it was time to grow some lady balls.

"So, um. Sorry to drop in like this, but I owe you a serious apology, and I wanted to deliver it in person." I leaned forward and put my hands on my bare knees to stop my sudden jimmy leg.

Brett finally looked back at me, his eyes a little squinty—from the sun or skepticism, I couldn't be sure. His lips shifted to the side before he spoke. "Nothing to apologize for."

I took a breath. "I was a jerk."

He shook his head. "No, you weren't. I get it, Liv. You had a rough day, to say the least, and then I—"

I cut him off, "You didn't do anything! I shouldn't have... I mean with Troy and me just—"

He raised a hand and it was his turn to cut me off. "I think we should just forget anything happened." He sighed and his hand fell back to his side. "And maybe we should avoid the topic of Troy altogether."

"You mean, just go back to before we..."

"Yeah."

I considered that. Could we do that, or would the whole incident on his couch always be between us? Did I even want to go back? I couldn't really think about that yet. The point was *he* clearly wanted to pretend we'd never crossed that line, so it wasn't really up to me anyway.

I forced a smile. "Okay. Sounds good to me."

He took a breath and let it out slowly. "Great."

We both fell silent and it was awkward as shit. Brett shifted on his feet after a minute, and I nodded my head as if answering some unspoken question. I had no fucking idea how to end this torture.

Suffering from the same predicament, Brett opened his mouth just as I did mine. His "I guess I'll talk to you later," and my, "I'll call you," collided and I felt my lips tip up in a genuine smile this time. His did as well.

Maybe I hadn't entirely ruined things after all.

"You're lying."

"I most certainly am not." I shook my head at Brett as I bent to tie my shoe, the sounds of early eighties rock punctuated by random crashes and bangs filling the air. "I'll even call her if you want me to."

He stood and studied me, clearly trying to determine if I was messing with him. I studied him from the corner of my eye in return, noting how unfair it was that Brett was the only person on earth who could actually make bowling shoes look cool. I was sure I looked like a clown in mine—and not the cool evil kind of clown, but your run-of-the-mill rent-a-clown variety.

While things between Brett and me had not been completely back to normal since that night in his apartment, they hadn't been nearly as awkward as I'd feared. After our friendship reboot in the parking lot of Centroe, we'd grabbed a quick drink and talked about absolutely nothing personal. It was a great start. And when he called to invite me to go bowling with the guys, I figured we were back in real friendship land. I refused to examine how I felt about that.

I sat up and pulled my phone from my pocket, hitting my mom's contact as soon as my thumb could locate it. I tapped the speaker button and her voicemail picked up.

"This is Meili. I'm not available at the moment, but please leave a message and I'll call you back."

I hung up before the beep and felt my mouth spread in a grin at Brett's dumbfounded expression. "The accent gets even more pronounced when she digs out her VHS player for an ONJ marathon." I cringed and shoved the phone back in my pocket. "God, she's made me watch that damn movie a hundred times."

"VHS I know, but ONJ?" Brett's friend Gavin interjected as he slid between us and placed his chosen ball in the metal return rack. I couldn't help but notice that he too suffered from the clown issue.

"Olivia Newton-John," Brett explained. "Liv's mom learned

English as a kid by watching *Grease* and listening to her music. She has an Australian accent."

Gavin's brows drew together as he shot a smartass glance at his best friend. "I'm told most people from Australia do."

"No. *Mrs. Sun* has an Australian accent. Not Olivia Newton-John. Well, she does too." Brett's tone was exasperated. "You know what I mean."

"Seriously?" Gavin tilted his head, his brown hair almost as messy as Brett's always was. He had a good four or five inches on Brett, and his general vibe was more cool jock than Brett's casual rocker meets lumbersexual. On paper, Gavin would have been just my type, yet I'd hardly given him a second glance since meeting him twenty minutes earlier. "Okay, *that's* weird." Gavin's brow furrowed.

"Believe me, I'm aware. What's arguably even more weird is that she had no problem giving her daughter the impression that a girl's virginity is a nuisance that should be dispensed with as soon as possible—preferably by dressing in black sparkly spandex and riding off with John Travolta to do the deed in a cloud."

Brett and Gavin both squinted at me. Clearly, they'd never seen *Grease*.

"What's virginity?" This came from Gavin's nephew who I'd kind of forgotten was within earshot. Oops.

"It has to do with God." Brett and Gavin responded simultaneously, and the boy, whose name was Rocco, just wrinkled his nose and went to pick out a bowling ball.

Brett answered my question before I could ask. "He hates going to church, so now whenever he asks a question that could get us in trouble with his mom, we just tell him it has to do with God. That way we know he'll never bring it up again."

I shook my head slowly. "There are so many things wrong with that, I don't even know where to start."

Brett just grinned and clapped his hands together. "You should be more worried about how badly you're gonna lose this game."

"You're so delusional it's almost adorable," I responded and strode away to pick out my own ball. It would have been perfect except for the fact that I almost slipped and fell on my ass with the damn bowling shoes. Brett's chuckle followed me and I intentionally ignored him.

Rocco was up first, and the automatic rails came up to keep his ball out of the gutter. He looked to be all of about seven and maybe fifty pounds with dark brown hair and eyes to match. And what he lacked in precision, he made up for in enthusiasm, cheering as his ball ping-ponged off the rails before finally taking down a couple pins. High fives were exchanged all around when he finished his turn with a seven.

Down went the rails and it was my turn. I wasn't the best bowler, but I've always been good under pressure so I wasn't too worried. I started with a split but managed to turn it into a spare with my second ball. I might have sashayed a bit on my way back to the seats while Gavin high fived me and Brett just gave me a careful appraisal. His serious expression had me laughing.

"Let me show you guys how it's done," Gavin taunted as he made a ridiculous show of preparing his throw. Rocco tossed his head back and laughed, revealing at least three missing teeth. Gavin got nine pins down on his first shot, but got too cocky on his second ball and landed it right in the gutter, much to Rocco's delight.

Brett didn't seem to notice any of it. He walked casually up to the lane with his ball, not bothering with any taunts. Reality was apparently hitting him and he could already see the writing on the wall. He pulled on the small plug in one of his earlobes and rocked his head from side to side before unceremoniously sending his ball straight down the center of the lane. The pins scattered as soon as the ball crashed into the first pin, securing a strike. Gavin groaned, Rocco cheered, and Brett silently turned back to us, shoving his hands in his front pockets like he hadn't just kicked our asses. Then his face slowly assumed the smuggest expression in human history as he swaggered so hard back to the seats I thought he might break a hip. I tried to look horrified, but my laughter broke through and I had to wipe my eyes by the time he sank into the seat next to me.

"You're an idiot." My stomach hurt from laughing so hard.

He winked at me, his lips parting to reveal his lopsided smile. My stomach pulled again, but this time it wasn't from laughter.

Me: How would you like to work on your pottery skills?

***Brett:** Is this a trick question?*

I grinned at my phone where it was balanced on the handle of my shopping cart.

Me: Maybe?

***Brett:** Explain yourself, woman.*

Me: I'm working on personal growth and I think you should join me. Throwing clay is very therapeutic, I'm told.

***Brett:** Not sure I'm in need of that kind of therapy, but you should totally go for it.*

I parked my cart by an endcap full of crackers and ran my thumbs over the phone.

Me: Please, for the love of God, you have to help me. I got roped into going to a pottery class by one of my clients and I need backup.

That's what I got for finally enacting my friend-making campaign. I was so not a pottery girl, but Angie and her adorable terrier mix had somehow managed to get me to agree to "unleash my inner potter" tomorrow night. I was more than a little terrified.

Brett: *As enjoyable as that sounds, I'm afraid I have to pass. I already made plans. And I'm not even lying.*

My heart sank more than it should have at that. We'd been hanging out and texting pretty regularly, and based on my inclusion in "guys' bowling," I knew where I stood. So, with this daunting therapeutic foray on the horizon I made a choice to chalk my disappointment up to fear and nothing more.

Me: *Okay. No biggie.*

Brett: *I'll be sure to clear my schedule for goat yoga if that's on the agenda next weekend.*

Me: *Haha. Thanks a lot.*

Brett: *Always. Talk to you later.*

I shoved my phone back in my pocket and pushed my shopping cart down the chips aisle, resisting the temptation to add numerous bags to my cart. Salad was what I needed. Not chips.

I was making some changes and eating healthier was on the list. Making better choices, in general, was the goal since I'd recently discovered I sometimes made really *really* shitty ones—like dating an asshole like Troy.

It was almost two weeks since Troy and I broke up—or rather, I stopped acknowledging his existence. As predicted, he'd tried his best to get back in my good graces, mostly just managing to contribute further evidence as to why I should have seen his douchey qualities for what they were in the first place.

Suffice it to say, Troy wasn't going down without a fight. He'd been less than pleased when he discovered I'd changed the locks, or so his banging on the door had indicated. Then he came and bugged me at work—several times—pissing me right the hell off. I mean, if he was having sex with other women, why did he want me back so badly? It made no sense to me. I know I'm considered kind of cute, but it's not like my vagina is made of gold or something. Since I didn't have an assistant in very often, he'd been able to corner me in my office. Thankfully I had a side door and could ditch him to call for reinforcements. On one occasion, when Joey showed up to help me out, Troy lit into him and I was afraid there'd be an outright brawl on the sidewalk outside my building. I'd had to install a doorbell on my own damn office after that. I was not letting my life go down that kind of reality-show spiral. I was better than that. Or at least I hoped I was.

So, on to salads it was. Just as I was patting myself on the back for making it to the produce section, my text notification sounded again. I figured it was Haley texting about the latest with Professor Nerdboy, but it was Brett again.

Brett: *Hey again. What's a good restaurant for a first date that's not too fancy? I'm shit at this kind of thing.*

My feet froze to the industrial flooring. I stared at the phone and swallowed hard, just as I felt the blood draining from my face. What was happening to me?

Rereading the message, I breathed deeply so I wouldn't do something stupid like pass out in the organic banana display at Lowes Foods. Brett was asking me for advice on where to take a woman for dinner.

And why shouldn't he? We were just friends after all. Nothing had happened between us that would indicate otherwise—or at least we were pretending it hadn't. I was beginning to suspect I was in a bit of trouble.

My thumbs felt detached from my body as they ran over the phone, typing a response the rest of me didn't want to give.

Me: *Lindley Park Filling Station is good, and it's pretty low-key.*

Brett: *Got it. Thanks!*

My response was automatic, but my heart thudded with each letter typed. An image of that Ginger girl materialized in my mind and I wanted to deflate her boobs with a pin.

Me: *Anytime.*

Brett was going out on a date tomorrow. And it wasn't with me. It was official. I was not only in trouble, I was in a waist-deep pile of *Oh Shit*. How I was going to fix this was a mystery to me. All I knew was the first step involved bypassing produce and heading right back to the chip aisle.

Chapter Eleven

NEGOTIATING THE BATTLEFIELD

RETT

"I can't believe he has a date."

I shushed Emerson and leaned into the counter. "Cut that shit out. The last thing a guy needs on the night of his first date is his sister blubbering all over him."

"I'm sorry, it's just a milestone and I'm happy for him. And nervous. What if she breaks his heart?" Her voice rose an octave.

"It's dinner. She won't have time to break anything." I shook my head and watched Emerson slice through an onion. She was cooking dinner for Gavin and me—probably to distract herself from her unhealthy obsession with the first event in her little brother's love life. Little did she know, a teenage boy's first love affair is between his dick and his hand. I was not going to be the one to bring that up, however.

But his sister's intense interest was exactly why Jay hadn't gone to her for advice, although asking me where to take a date was far from the best idea. I hung out at Jake's, which he well knew. But, considering he was in high school, a bar wasn't an option—unless he wanted his date's parents to end his budding baseball career with a broken arm or two. Luckily, Liv had come up with a great suggestion and Jay was set for the evening.

Meanwhile, I was struggling like hell over the whole Liv thing. Part of me was glad to have her back as my friend—one I could call on for such things as dating advice for my young friend. But the other part longed for more. Much more. That part was screaming at me to go get her and damn the consequences.

When she'd shown up at my office last week, I hadn't known what to expect. I was tempted to pretend I hadn't seen her in case she was there to tell me she was leaving town or getting back together with Troy Assface. But as soon as the words "I'm sorry" had left her mouth, all I could think was how I wanted to preserve anything I could with her—even if that meant I'd never taste her again or feel the heated center of her pushing down on me again. Or get the chance to stare at her naked for an hour or ten like I so desperately wanted.

I didn't want her regretting our encounter. I also didn't want her regretting ever meeting me. But I couldn't put myself in a position to be just some guy she had a fling with once.

From the corner of my eye, I spotted the tall figure hugging the hallway wall in an attempt to sneak by unnoticed. I bit the inside of my cheek to hide my smile and figured I'd do the kid a favor. "Is that a new picture?" I pointed behind Emerson and she turned to look at the photo I'd indicated. I glanced over my own shoulder and saw Jay give me a chin lift before slinking out the front door.

Emerson turned back, her auburn hair swinging. "You've seen

that picture a hundred times." The unmistakable sound of a car engine turning over called from outside and her jaw dropped. "I can't believe you!" She threw a kitchen towel at me and I couldn't do anything but laugh.

"If you piss her off, she may not cook for you. Just a word of advice." Gavin wandered into the kitchen and dropped a brief kiss on Emerson's lips.

"You should listen to him. He knows what he's talking about." She pointed her knife at me and I threw my hands up in surrender.

"Sorry, but us single dudes have to stick together."

Gavin chuckled and headed to the fridge. "Jay could do a lot worse, I guess. Let him stay and eat, Ace."

"Fine. But I'm getting the recap when Jay comes home, and you can't stop me." She lifted her chin and gave me what I assumed was her best hard-ass lawyer stare-down.

Jay was staying with his sister while his parents were out of town for some hippy craft show or something. I wasn't about to break it to her that he'd be even more scarce once he got home. Instead, I let her believe what she wanted, as long as it got me a home-cooked meal.

"Have at it," I responded, and she went back to her chopping.

I thought we were done, but her knife paused on the cutting board. "You know, you're always welcome to invite a friend along when you come over."

Gavin groaned from where he had his head stuck in the refrigerator.

"Uh. Okay."

She set the knife down again. "It's just that I haven't heard you mention anyone since your friend with the cheating boyfriend."

"What's with all the meddling? That's more Fiona's style."

Gavin reinstated himself in the position of my best friend by going on the defensive for me.

Emerson shook her head, looking a bit horrified. "Oh, God. She's rubbing off on me." Her mouth turned down and she put both hands flat on the counter. "Sorry, Brett."

I waved her off. I hadn't mentioned Liv or the fallout from the whole Troy thing to anyone but Gavin, and the last thing I needed was to be roped into another pow-wow with the women and their endless efforts at "helping"—or what us lay people refer to as "interfering." For all they knew, Liv was completely off my radar. They couldn't be more wrong.

An hour later, with a belly full of flank steak and roasted vegetables, I sat on Emerson's deck with a beer in front of me and Gavin sitting across the table. Emerson always had ten things going on at once, and tonight was no different. Through the glass patio doors, I could see her on the couch inside, phone to one ear and laptop open on the coffee table.

Gavin followed my gaze. "It's like we're nothing but a dryer full of socks and it's their sworn duty to find a match for every last one," he said. "They're after Ari now. I think they're trying to set her up with Jax."

"Jesus. Poor bastard won't know what hit him."

Emerson's friend Ari was... well, she was a lot of things, but an easygoing girlfriend, I imagined, was not one of those things.

"Isn't she always dating assholes, though? That would kind of rule Jax out." He was Fiona's boss, a completely laid-back guy and, by my calculations, about ten years older than Ari.

Gavin tossed his bottle cap in a perfect arc into the stone firepit off the deck. "As far as I can tell. What is it that makes some girls always choose assholes? I mean, I can tell right off the bat if some-one's an asshole. It's not rocket science."

I shifted in my chair. "The same reason I always date shallow women and cheaters, I guess." It seemed Liv and I had our terrible taste in significant others in common, at least.

Gavin lifted his beer and pointed it at me. "Not any more, though."

"Yeah." Not that I was likely to date anyone in the near future, with Liv on my mind. And in my phone. And sitting next to me at the bowling alley. It wasn't like I resented her for not returning my feelings. And I could probably have worked my way into becoming her rebound guy, but I was over being a doormat. That was the old Brett. "Never again." And I meant it.

"Liv still have you friend-zoned?"

"Firmly." I took a swig of my beer.

"Sorry, man." Gavin leaned back in his chair.

I looked around at the expensive deck furniture and perfectly landscaped backyard and wondered again how in the hell my best friend had scored a successful lawyer five years his senior. I was happy for him, no doubt about it, but I admit I was more than a little jealous of their easy relationship.

"Yeah. The thing is, I'd rather hang out with her as a friend than not hang out with her at all. If that's all I can get, I'll take it." I took another pull on my beer, the cold liquid running a soothing path down my suddenly dry throat.

"Shit." Gavin set his bottle on the table with a clang.

"What?"

"That means it's worse than I thought."

What in the hell was I supposed to say to that? He was absolutely right. At this rate, I'd never get laid again. I silently apologized to my dick and thought about getting drunk.

"Okay, let's go." Gavin pushed his chair back and stood.

"Where are we going?"

"Where do you think?"

Now this was the kind of therapy I could get on board with. I relaxed my stance and adjusted my grip, waiting for the release. The machine clattered, the sound echoing in the open air just before the ball came hurtling toward me. I brought the bat around and connected, sending the ball into the pad at the end of the cage with a *thwack*.

It had been way too long since I'd made the time to hit the cages, and it was just like Gavin to know where to go tonight. Since we were fourteen, we'd been hitting balls while swapping stories and insults, talking about girls, and bragging about more than a few fictitious conquests. Not that we didn't always know the other one was full of shit, but it was part of being best friends.

"Damn, that was a nice one." Gavin tipped his helmet to me.

It wasn't often I impressed anyone with my playing skills. "Fuck off. Stop pandering."

"I'm not pandering." Gavin grunted as he hit his next ball.

"Yes you are. And if you don't focus, you're gonna take a pitch in the face and I'll have to explain to your girlfriend why you're ugly as fuck."

As good a friend as Gavin was, it was no secret that he'd always been the star and I'd been the sidekick. And that was okay. I never had the need to be the center of attention, and I was grateful for what life had thrown my way. For the most part. But it sure would feel good to not just have something good, but something fucking amazing. Something that was mine and mine alone. Maybe that was why the Liv thing was hitting me so hard. I felt in my gut that she and I could have that.

I didn't notice that Gavin had flipped his switch off and was facing me through the cage until he rose his voice. "Hey."

"What?" I tapped the plate with my bat.

"Anybody ever tell you you have a selective memory?"

I looked at him curiously, wondering if he had, indeed, taken one to the head and I'd just missed it. He gripped the chain-link fence with his free hand, letting me know he wasn't done talking. I ignored him and swung at my next pitch. I caught it low and it popped up, making me duck while Gavin stood perfectly still, not even twitching.

"I know exactly what you're thinking, man," he continued. I stood upright again and flipped my switch to off. If he was insisting on gabbing like a teenage girl, I wasn't about to get knocked out while he did it. "Do I need to remind you exactly how much of a loser I was a few years back?"

I leaned on my bat, feeling a bead of sweat drip down my neck from beneath my helmet. Now that he mentioned it, though, he had been kind of pathetic for a while there. Not that I really blamed him. He'd been on his way to the majors when he fucked his arm up and kind of fell off the deep end.

He pulled his fingers from the fence and pointed at his chest. "I was a quitter. Plain and simple." His finger changed directions to pin me. "You never quit. Not once have I seen you give up on something."

What was this, a pick-me-up speech from my dad? "Thanks, Pops. I'll file that away."

"Asshole." Gavin grinned at me. "Seriously, though. You pulled me out of my personal two-year pity party, and I won't ever forget that. You wouldn't let me quit, and I sure as hell won't let you."

I eyed him and raised a brow. "Is there a moral to this story, or do I have to guess?"

He flipped me off.

"You need to treat this friend-zone thing as just a temporary setback. You may have lost the battle, but you're winning the fucking war, my friend. Liv's not gonna know what hit her."

At the confident tone and eager look on his face, I busted out laughing. Gavin didn't even have the grace to look chagrinned. Eventually, I just shook my head and we both got back up to the plate and crushed some more pitches. Because this was baseball, and it was sacred.

She was impossible to miss. Not only because of her bright smile and the smooth golden skin bared by her off-the-shoulder top, but because she was the only person in the lobby with a two-hundred-pound Great Dane at her side.

I felt my own returning smile grow as I walked toward her.

She bit her lip when I got close. "Sorry, but I had to bring him. It's too hot to leave him in the car."

I chuckled while she gave small self-conscious waves to the passersby as they eyed her and Tambo curiously. "It's no problem. It's my fault for catching you on such short notice. Thanks again for doing this."

A team of us had been working around the clock on this pitch we had to give to a visiting marketing executive tomorrow, and we'd found ourselves stuck on a particular issue that involved the touchy subject of animal testing. The group was split on including aspects of it in our presentation, and we were running out of time. It had occurred to me this afternoon that Liv might be able to shed some light, being the most expert voice on animals I knew. So, she'd agreed to stop in and take a look as soon as I called her.

"Come on." I motioned for her and Tambo to follow me to a conference room down the hall. A massive table occupied the space, every inch of the surface covered in papers, photos, empty coffee cups, and even a couple dozing heads of team members.

"Everyone, this is Dr. Olivia Sun. Liv, this is everyone." I gestured to the team of exhausted and rumpled office slaves.

She received some hellos and waves, which she returned, but Tambo got the majority of the group's attention, which he lapped up like he'd been neglected for days. "So, what's the deal?" Liv dove right in.

I gestured to a chair. "It's the nature of the testing we're not sure of. As you're aware, animal testing is not a new thing, and given its polarizing nature among potential customers, we need to pinpoint exactly what some of this verbiage refers to." I showed her the pages of documentation we had, which read like Greek to all of us. There was a reason we were in marketing and not research. A lot of our material was proprietary, but these reports were a matter of public record, so involving an outsider was no big deal. The fact that she also happened to be the object of my horny fantasies was something I'd be keeping from my fellow team members.

She took a seat and flipped the first page over. I watched as she scanned it and moved to the next page. Her lips moved as she read, and the slight motion captivated me. All I could remember was those same lips on mine. How she tasted, how she sounded when she moaned into my mouth.

Fuck. I had to stop this before I embarrassed myself at work. I needed sleep. I needed coffee. I probably needed to rub one out when I got home too.

"Okay, here." Liv pointed to a spot halfway down the page and turned her eyes to me. I blinked and managed to tear my gaze from her mouth to meet her eyes. Was it my imagination, or did some color rise to her cheeks? I was going crazy. She cleared her throat and began again. "Here. This sentence explains some of the extent of testing." She continued to talk and read, explaining along the way exactly what the lab was doing. By the time she was done, we were relieved to find the testing was minimal and noninvasive. The executive wouldn't need to be bothered with it and we could keep it out of our proposal.

Everyone thanked Liv and I walked her and her dog out to the parking lot. It was after five and the lot was emptying out, cars maneuvering their way around us. I pulled her to the side. "You're a life saver. We're all brain dead and that was the last piece."

"Anytime." She smiled and pulled Tambo closer with his leash.

"I'll buy you dinner or something to say a more proper thanks." Without thinking, I continued, "Maybe I'll take you to Lindley Park Filling Station." I inwardly cringed, realizing too late that it sounded like I was asking her out on a date when we'd agreed on being just friends.

And from the responding look on her face, she'd clearly come to the same conclusion. If I wasn't mistaken, her expression was almost one of horror before she schooled it and stepped back. Ouch. She pulled on Tambo's leash and mustered a lackluster smile. "I gotta go. Good luck with the presentation."

So much for winning that war. I'm not sure she could have retreated faster if I were offering up a smallpox-ridden blanket instead of dinner. Shit.

Chapter Twelve

THERE'S NEVER A SHARPIE OR A MAINTENANCE CLOSET AROUND WHEN YOU NEED ONE

 IV

"I get it if you don't want to come."

I tossed the t-shirt in the cardboard box and glared at Joey. "I'm coming. I already missed enough games trying to avoid Troy, I'm not missing this one."

I'd skipped the three home games I could have attended, not wanting to lay eyes on Troy's stupid face, but it was time to get over myself and support my cousin and my team. I wasn't letting Troy take that away from me. He may have stolen some of my dignity, but he wasn't getting baseball too.

A stainless-steel water bottle and a *Men's Health* magazine went in the box next. I peeked up at Joey and saw him rubbing the back of his neck, his forehead creased and mouth turned down. He looked tired. And he needed a haircut before people started mistaking him for Asian Jesus.

Although Joey refused to talk about it, I gathered the Troy situation was making things rough on the field as well. When I tried mentioning it, he always brushed it aside, but numbers don't lie, and the team had taken a hit since Troy and Joey had butted heads over me.

It was time for me to fix it, and if that meant pretending things with Troy were old news or water under the bridge, I'd do it for Joey. And the truth was, I didn't give a shit about Troy anymore. Sure, it sucks to be lied to and cheated on, but at least I found out sooner rather than later so I could move the hell on. The only real feelings I had left for the guy were anger and a strong inclination to kick him in the balls.

"Are these yours or his?" I held up a pair of socks for Joey to inspect.

"His," he responded. "I haven't asked you to do my laundry all season." My cousin sounded oddly impressed with himself, as if doing your own laundry was an accomplishment worthy of public praise.

The socks went in the box along with all the other odds and ends of Troy's that I'd been collecting. I'd thought about throwing it all in the trash but decided to try and be mature about it instead. That didn't mean I might not draw a big penis in Sharpie on the outside of the box, though. I was feeling particularly salty toward Troy since I'd gone to get tested this morning and was waiting on my results. Haley had wanted to go with me, but I couldn't stand to wait any longer.

Joey picked up a veterinary journal from my coffee table and started mindlessly flipping through it. "I'm actually kind of nervous." He gave a self-deprecating grunt. "And you know I don't get that way often."

It was true. Joey was always a cool customer on the field, but Saturday was going to be a big night. There had been some rumblings about the starting shortstop for the Black Dogs, and with the Guardians being one of their farm teams, there was a good chance Joey could be called up. He'd been on fire all week on the field, but Saturday would be the first game in their next series against the Lancers, who were tough as hell.

There were no two ways about it. I'd be at Saturday's game cheering Joey on with everything I had. Thankfully, I'd have Haley by my side to make our cheering twice as loud.

"Hey." I grabbed his attention. "It's okay to be nervous, but you're gonna kick ass. And then I'll be watching you on TV all summer." I grinned and pumped my fists like a weirdo.

He laughed, so I got the reaction I wanted. I scanned the floor to see if I'd missed anything and then folded the flaps on the box. "Hand me that tape, will you?" Joey passed over the packing tape and I secured the flaps. "You don't have to talk to him, but maybe you could just drop the box by his locker or something?" Troy had moved out of their shared apartment, but they obviously still shared a locker room. I didn't know where Troy was staying now and I didn't ask.

"Yeah, sure." Joey eyed me again.

"I'm totally fine. I promise." I put my hands out, as if my true feelings had been hiding out behind my back.

"I'm allowed to worry." He dropped the journal back down on the glass surface.

"I know. And I appreciate it, but I'm ready to move on." I regretted the words as soon as they left my mouth, so I went in search of that Sharpie, hoping Joey would let it go.

No such luck.

"Move on, as in, halt all plans of homicide? Or, as in, date someone else? That someone being your buddy, Brett."

"Sorry, what?" I dug through the kitchen junk drawer, pretending I hadn't heard him. I bent and tilted my head down, making a real show of it by shoving the drawer's contents around and making a racket.

"You heard me."

I jumped and turned around. Joey had snuck up behind me and scared the shit out of me.

The image of Brett standing outside the Centroe building inviting me to the same restaurant he'd taken that Ginger chick or some other date to the previous weekend made my breakfast threaten to reappear. I mean, even if his date had gone horribly—which I secretly hoped it had—just the thought of being one in a continuing line of first dates was downright depressing. His wince of regret after asking me also hadn't gone unnoticed. But he didn't have to worry about me reading anything into his invitation. I knew where I stood.

I jabbed Joey with an elbow. "Help me find a Sharpie."

"You didn't answer my question." He boxed me in, his eight-inch height advantage making it particularly effective.

"Fine. I'm not killing anyone, and maybe I have a miniscule hint of a crush on Brett. But it doesn't matter, because Troy and I broke up five minutes ago, and I think Brett's dating someone." I tried not to let my feelings about that show, so I hurried on, "Now help me find a damn Sharpie so I can draw a diseased penis on Troy's box."

Joey laughed in my face. "I knew it!"

"You knew what? That I can draw a penis? I am a doctor, you know."

He shook his head, taking a step back. "How old are you?"

I smacked his arm and slid past him, but he just followed me back to the living room. "From what I could tell, you don't have to worry about another girl. That guy is… well, let's just say it's clear he cares about you."

I stopped with my back to Joey. Brett did care about me. I knew that. It was one of the reasons I'd felt so bad that I jumped him that night. But I didn't think Brett would ever believe that I wanted to explore something between us with this whole Troy thing still hanging out there. I wasn't a safe bet and I knew it. The fact that my hands went numb every time I thought about him kissing another woman was something I'd have to ignore.

"Yeah, well, we're friends. And that's really okay, Joey. I probably should be on my own for a while anyway."

The problem was the memory of kissing him and the feel of his skin against my fingers and his cock grinding into me made it very hard to settle for just friends. I'd been so turned on that night, despite the inappropriateness of it all. Sometimes I could still feel his beard brushing my cheek and neck as his lips traced a path over my skin.

I had to stop thinking about this, especially with Joey in the room. I pasted a smile on and turned to him. "I have to take Tambo out. Thanks for delivering the box."

Saturday's game was a hot fucking mess, and it was all my fault. Thank God Haley was there to keep me from losing my shit.

It started well enough, the teams taking the field in turn and warming up. I noticed Troy and Joey kept their distance from one another, a stark contrast to their usual back slapping and fist bumping. But as long as neither of them was being combative, I figured it was just the way it would be. You didn't have to be BFFs with everyone on your team to play together. My hope was that they could put their differences aside for the sake of the game they both loved.

But if I'd had inklings of the discord affecting the team before, it was proven in the first inning. Joey stopped a line drive and threw it to first for the out, and as the crowd cheered, I noticed Troy mouthing something to my cousin. Thankfully, Joey seemed to ignore him. Then when the inning turned over, Troy blatantly checked him with his shoulder on the way back to the dugout. It was like six-year-olds on the playground. Again, Joey ignored him, but every muscle in my body was strung tight by that point.

And, although Joey let it go, it didn't go unnoticed by a couple other players who then got in Troy's face. He shoved one of them before the coaches ordered them all to get their asses in the dugout.

Right then and there, I swore to myself if Troy ruined Joey's chances of moving up, I would rip his balls off and shove them down his throat.

"I don't think I can look. What's happening now?" My face rested on my palms and my elbows were propped on my knees.

"Ummm. The other team's pitcher keeps shaking his head. Looks like some kind of facial tic—or maybe water in his ears?"

I uncovered one eye and tilted my head to narrow it at Haley.

"What?" When I didn't answer she shrugged. At the sound of a ball connecting with wood, I had to squeeze my elbows into my sides to keep myself from looking. "Oh!" Haley's tone was excited. "Oh." It quickly switched to disappointed. "He's out."

I couldn't get through a whole game like this, but it was better than the cringe-worthy beginning. It was the bottom of the third and we'd already changed seats to the upper deck to distance ourselves after Troy kept throwing weird smirks our way—clearly in the middle of some kind of mental breakdown. The Guardians were up at bat, so I was waiting for Joey's turn before I dared to watch. We had a player on second, I knew, and Joey would be up soon.

"Uh, Liv," Haley poked me in the shoulder.

"I'm not looking."

"Liv." Another poke.

"Just tell me when it's Joey's turn."

"Liv." That most definitely was not Haley's voice this time.

My resolve flew out the window and my head shot up to find Brett MacKinnon standing just to the other side of Haley, looking all kinds of delicious with his plain black t-shirt, worn jeans, Chucks, and a sexy-ass grin. Despite the awful game, I felt my mouth break into a dopey smile. "Hi."

I watched as his eyes dropped to my mouth and his grin turned into a full-fledged, pearly-white showcase of a perfectly lopsided smile. My heart thrummed and I bit my lip to keep myself from blurting out something embarrassing like, "Can I please sit on your lap?"

My relief that the weirdness from our last encounter had faded was a leaden weight off my chest, and I couldn't quite remember why it was a bad thing that he'd asked me to dinner. In fact, I was thinking I'd love nothing better than to go to dinner with him right freaking now. I'm not sure how long we smiled at each other in silence before Haley interrupted, but it was certainly long enough that we both should have been blushing. Instead, I didn't give a good goddamn.

"So… hi?" Haley put a hand out toward Brett and it broke the moment. This was not my first rodeo, so I can tell you with not a small degree of certainty that the look in Brett's eyes was not a *let's just be friends* look. It definitely read more like something in the neighborhood of *let's go find a maintenance closet and fuck.* Dare I say my heart was aflutter at that?

Brett, clearly having more access to his brain cells than me, took Haley's hand with a less naughty grin. "Hi. Brett. I'm a friend of Liv's." He nodded as I silently tacked a little something on to the end of his sentence for him. *But I'm hoping to make her more than my friend as soon as fucking possible. And, by the way, my date last weekend was a hideous beast.*

Haley's voice came out overly loud when she answered, "Well, hello, BRRREETTT," eying me pointedly as she added a half dozen syllables to his name. I fought an eyeroll. "It's so nice to meet you." She shot him a sugary smile and gestured to the empty spot next to me, making sure to give me a less-than-subtle wide-eyed glance while she was at it. "Join us!"

Brett's eyes came to me again, searching my features. I nodded and something passed over his face before his mouth relaxed into an easy smile again. "Sure. Just for a bit, though. I'm here with some friends." He gestured behind him and Haley and I both craned our necks, as if his friends would all conveniently be wearing hats emblazoned with "Brett's Friends" just for our benefit.

But, shit. It was impossible *not* to spot them immediately. They were the only ten people not watching the field, but instead apparently riveted by Brett's and our exchange. Good grief. Brett looked over his shoulder and did a double take, finally turning back to us with a sheepish expression.

My gaze involuntarily shot back to his friends. It was a mixed crowd of men and women, most of whom had thankfully returned their attention to the game. But there were two women still turned our way. One was a petite blonde wearing an amused expression.

The other was a busty, lustrous-haired, Latina goddess shooting daggers directly my way. I swallowed hard and felt my stomach drop. It seemed I'd just gotten my first look at Brett's dinner date. She wasn't Ginger and she wasn't a hideous beast. And if I read her expression right, she'd be busy slashing my tires during the seventh inning stretch.

Chapter Thirteen

NEVER APOLOGIZE FOR BEING A BAD-ASS

RETT

I was going to kill those assholes.

Despite Gavin's plans for all-out warfare in the name of love, I'd laid a bit low since Liv and Tambo's retreat from my dinner invitation. Our work presentation had gone well, but it meant we were moving on with the project, all cylinders firing. I'd dragged my ass home exhausted the last few nights. I hadn't texted or talked to Liv, and I knew her friend Haley was coming to town this weekend, so part of me was just waiting for things to blow over. And my pride to recover. But when the guys had insisted we all go to the Saturday night Guardians game, I couldn't refuse. Both because it was an early summer game night and because I had a guess Liv would be there and I couldn't seem to help my damn self.

It had taken all of about thirty seconds to spot her in her usual seat in section 104. I had zero intention of letting anyone in my group know she was there, but I discovered I'm shit at covert surveillance. All it took was me missing a perfect catch from our left fielder for Gavin to identify my distraction. From there, it was no use trying to keep it under wraps. The news traveled through our group like a bad case of herpes at Coachella. Comments ranged from "She's hot" to "I wonder where she got those shoes," while I pretended I didn't know any of these people sitting with me.

But everything came to a halt when Troy Assface behaved in a manner true to his name—or, well, my name for him—and started messing with Liv's cousin.

"Did you see that?" Nate asked.

I watched as a couple of our players got in Horner's face for being a dick and a coach put an end to it. What the fuck was wrong with this guy?

Gavin watched quietly and didn't comment. Neither did I.

"Is that the cheating dirtbag? Eww." That one came from Laney who was sitting next to Nate.

Ari leaned over Gavin to look at me. As usual, she was dressed in a low-cut top that left little to the imagination and I had to shift my focus to her forehead to avoid getting a full-on view down her generous cleavage to her belly button. "There's something seriously wrong with that guy."

She didn't need to tell me.

I tried to ignore Troy and enjoy the game, cheering with the crowd as we struck out one of the Lancers' best players and partaking in the beers and classic stadium fare from the vendor roaming our section. The weather was beautiful and the sun hung low and bright in the sky. But something was missing.

Liv wasn't shouting—neither with cheers nor insults. Instead, she and her friend with the red-blond hair simply leaned into one another, exchanging comments and only glancing at the field. It felt all kinds of wrong.

When the Guardians took the field again, Horner made a detour to pass close to the foul line, putting himself within a few yards of Liv. He tipped his hat and sent her a smile I assumed was supposed to be confident, but to me it came off creepy as hell. Not that I was biased or anything.

"You've got to be kidding me," Ari grumbled while I maintained my silence and tried to focus on the game. She shook her head. "Well, I'm hitting the ladies. Anybody else need to go?" Emerson and Laney joined her, and we all shifted to let them by and out into the aisle.

We managed to close the inning out without letting the Lancers get a man past second. But it didn't escape my notice that, once again, Troy made a point to single Liv out with a beckoning smile on his way back to the dugout. I looked at Gavin and found his eyes following Troy's movements as well. I just shook my head.

This was a big fucking problem.

Let me explain.

If anyone could distract me from imminent death by an oncoming tractor trailer, it would be Olivia Sun. I'd be a stain on I-40 before you could blink. But a baseball player who was shooting for the majors didn't get distracted. His focus was always on the game. He didn't search his ex-girlfriend out in the stands, he didn't pick fights with his own teammates, and he most certainly didn't let his coaches and managers witness him doing either one. But there he was, acting like the biggest moron on earth and jeopardizing his career because, *what*—his girlfriend caught him cheating? He got a well-deserved broken nose? This guy was fucking crazy.

Just before the start of the third inning, I noticed Liv and her friend leave their seats. I assumed they were headed to the restrooms, but when they didn't come back, I felt my mood plummet further. I hadn't even talked to the woman, yet her presence among a few thousand other people in this huge space had made my chest warm. I suppose I couldn't really blame her for leaving, though, with the weirdness that was Troy.

Emerson, Laney, and Ari returned, whispering heatedly about some girl shit I couldn't make out and didn't care to. Ari seemed particularly worked up as we all shifted to let them back to their seats. Emerson was shaking her head and, if I wasn't mistaken, threatening to slit her friend's throat. *Okay.* Visits to the men's room never ended with death threats, that's all I can say.

While I was shifting to let them by, my eye caught on a cascade of dark shiny hair in the next section. My mouth spread in a grin as I recognized Liv in her Guardians jersey and ball cap. She and her friend hadn't left after all. They'd just put a little distance between themselves and the mental case on second.

Before I knew what I was doing, I was out of my seat and headed her way. When I approached, I almost laughed at the sight of her burying her face in her hands as her friend gave her the play-by-play. Haley finally noticed me and I saw her trying to work out if I was drunk, lost, or just a run-of-the-mill creeper before she nudged Liv to get her attention.

"Just tell me when it's Joey's turn."

When I smiled at that, Haley seemed to realize I knew Liv and wasn't a credible threat. She poked her again, but I cut in.

"Liv."

Liv's head popped up and her wide eyes locked on mine, sending a flash through my groin and a punch to my solar plexus. When she hit me with an automatic smile—generous, joyful, and so damn beautiful—I couldn't help but smile back with everything I had. My relief was profound, as was my desire to kiss her sweet mouth.

Introductions were made and I eventually dropped in the seat beside Liv. Both Haley and my parade of idiot friends were painfully obvious in their curiosity, making me think perhaps they all needed to get laid if they found watching Liv and me make small talk so fucking fascinating.

It didn't go unnoticed by Liv, and she shot several glances to my crew, her expression indiscernible. I didn't know if it had to do with the attention we were garnering, a return of her discomfort with my presence, or the fact that Troy was probably scanning the crowd from the dugout searching for her.

But before things could get too weird, Joey was up at bat. I'd been following his stats even though I hadn't been to any games with my work craziness. He was on a streak that surely had him exercising every superstition a player might have—I wouldn't have been surprised to learn he'd been wearing the same unwashed socks for the last two weeks and hadn't stepped on a single side-walk crack in all that time.

The first pitch was high and just outside, drawing a ball. The second was straight down the middle and that was all she wrote. The bat connected with a deafening crack, and the ball sailed straight past the Lancers' pitcher and second baseman while Joey ran like a bat out of hell, rounding first and making it safely to second before the Lancers could gain control and get the ball back infield. Our guy who'd been on second sprinted safely over home plate and the Guardians were up by one. We were out of our seats, screaming our heads off, fists in the air. And that was how I found myself with two arms full of gorgeous green-clad woman as Liv executed a haphazard, if not enthusiastic, leap, wrapping her arms around my neck and her legs around my waist and screaming in my ear. Sort of like a loud, sexy monkey with a proclivity for spontaneous trust falls.

Not wanting to drop her, I grabbed the first thing I could find for purchase, which just happened to be both of her firm asscheeks encased in cut-off shorts that had ridden up in her exuberance. My fingers clasped on the exposed skin of her upper thighs while she continued to smile and yell Joey's name. I let out a groan, but it was drowned out by the noise. In any other situation, a woman in my arms calling out another man's name would kill the mood in an instant, but this was one situation where I could make an exception. Especially when she bent and planted a short, hard kiss on my mouth. Haley started hugging us both while she jumped around, and I had to let Liv down before I hauled her out of the stadium and back to my car. But I gave her ass one last squeeze before I let her shoes hit the ground. I'm only a man, after all.

And that man is no idiot, so I wasn't letting myself read too much into that kiss, as much as I enjoyed it. People do things in the heat of the moment when their adrenaline is running high, and for all I knew, she didn't even realize she'd done it. Still smiling, we all calmed the hell down and turned our attention back to the game.

Liv clenched her fists in excitement. "I'm so happy for him!" I watched her smile as the setting sun played over her freckles. Her head snapped to me. "What do you think? Does he have a shot at Ramirez's spot?"

She was talking about the shortstop for our affiliated majors team, the Black Dogs, who was nursing a bad knee and in need of some downtime. "I'd take him if I were the Black Dogs. Numbers don't lie."

Her smile was downright dazzling and I wanted her to put those soft lips on mine again. But there was baseball to watch and a crowd surrounding us. Our next player came up to the plate and Liv's eyes dropped to her lap.

"Uh, sorry about that, by the way."

"Huh?"

She glanced up at me for a second before letting her eyes wander to the crowd. Her cheeks colored. "The, uh, the kissing thing."

"Oh." I started and shook my head, trying to think of how to respond. Her mouth turned down and it seemed her good mood was on the decline. That was the last thing I wanted. "Never, ever, apologize for kissing a guy. That's like Bruce Lee apologizing for being a complete badass." That got a bit of a grin, just like I'd intended. "And, besides, I'm going to start getting a complex if you apologize every time you lay a hand—or any other body part —on me."

She laughed this time, but her gaze went over my shoulder again and she shifted in her seat. I turned to find my group of assholes, but nobody seemed to be paying any attention to us. God, I hated this uncertainty between us. We needed to clear the air once and for all. But this was not the time or place, I was reminded as I caught Haley's wink over Liv's shoulder. Jesus.

We relaxed in our seats again, chatting and watching as the Guardians fought a difficult battle onfield. It was easy to see why Haley and Liv were friends, as they both shared a similar sense of humor and a clear affection for one another. And Haley further endeared herself to me by looking like she might vomit every time Troy executed a solid play. Which wasn't as often as the team needed, unfortunately. It didn't escape my attention that he was favoring his throwing arm, subtle as he was about it. But combine that with his outward aggression to his teammates and his distraction by Liv's presence and the guy was a mess. Again, I was struck with his seemingly casual attitude toward what was essentially his future in baseball.

Liv and Haley eventually gave in to go break the seal and I wandered back to my group in the meantime. Half of them had apparently had the same need for the facilities, but it didn't stop the rest of them from giving me shit about Liv. I believe the least obnoxious comment came from Fiona who instructed me to "go fill Liv out like an application."

I was just about to go back to find Liv and Haley when Ari, having returned from the bathroom, wedged her way between me and Gavin. As soon as she raised her finger, I knew I was in trouble.

"I'm sorry, but I can't stay silent about this. You're a man of few words and I don't quite get this whole thing you have going on," she gestured up and down my bearded face and casual outfit before continuing, "but I like you. You're a good guy."

"Um, thanks?" I had zero clue where she was going with this, yet my palms began to sweat.

"So I feel a responsibility to let you know that your *girl*," She threw a thumb over her shoulder, clearly indicating Liv, "is padding her squeaky-clean-I'm-a-doctor-and-I'm-so-cute-and-perky bank account with the proceeds from her side business selling illegal prescription drugs with her *boyfriend*." She swung a finger to the field where Troy Horner strutted out to second base looking like the absolute asshole I knew him to be.

Oh, for fuck's sake.

Chapter Fourteen

SOFIA VERGARA HAS SOME EXPLAINING TO DO

IV

It was a miracle I didn't wet myself. And not because I'd waited too long to use the restroom.

"Holy crap!" Haley checked the women's room door to make sure the coast was clear and then came closer to inspect my face. "Who was that?"

I'm sure I was ghost white, having just been dressed down by a very beautiful, very scary, Latina goddess. The same one who had been giving me death glares since Brett found us earlier in the evening.

"Um, I'm pretty sure that was Brett's new girlfriend if her threat to pull my fingernails off with rusty pliers if I didn't stay away from him was anything to go by."

I'd been waiting by the sinks for Haley to finish in the bathroom when the woman from Brett's group had materialized out of nowhere and thrown that psycho threat in my face. She kept her voice low, but it was a burning fire of fury with a glare to match it. I'd been so shocked I hadn't been able to utter a word. Not to mention I was busy choking on my own tongue.

Apart from the mentally unhinged part, it was easy to see why Brett—or any man—would be all over this woman. She had an incredible set of boobs, a tiny waist, and gorgeous hair and skin. If I weren't terrified, I'd probably have a crush on her too.

"No way! Seriously?" Haley's eyes shot to the door again and she looked like she was contemplating going after the girl.

I grabbed her arm. "Don't! You're pretty much my only friend and I can't have your death on my conscience." I wouldn't be surprised to find that the new girl had dug a shallow grave or two in her day.

Haley narrowed her eyes. "This is ridiculous. If Brett were dating her, he wouldn't have been sitting there eye-humping you for the last hour. You must have misunderstood." She turned one of the taps on and ran her hands under the water.

There weren't too many ways to interpret the whole fingernail thing, but she did have a small point. "You think he was eye-humping me?" I tried to quell the hopefulness in my tone. It didn't work.

She flipped off the tap. "No. I'm pretty sure he was mentally calculating all the ways he wants to put his P in your V if I'm being honest, but I was trying to be polite." Her grin was downright naughty.

Despite the looks I got from that girl while we watched the game with Brett, I'd tried to convince myself she didn't mean anything to him, just like Haley implied. I even considered that maybe her sworn enemy was sitting in the row behind us and the glare was meant for that poor soul instead of me. I mean, Brett spent half the game flirting and talking to me, so that had to mean something, right? And that crazy attraction wasn't in my imagination, nor was our gut-level connection. Brett got me, and I'd never met anyone in my life I'd had such an immediate connection with. But regardless of Brett's true feelings toward that woman, *her* feelings were crystal clear.

I took a breath and shook my head. "Well, either way I can't go back out there. I like my fingernails exactly where they are."

Haley's shoulders slumped and she put on a pout. "But you guys are so cute together."

I kind of thought so too, but I had to be careful—both with my heart and my fingernails. "Yeah, well, so are Brett and Sofia Vergara's younger, more well-endowed sister." I grabbed Haley by the arms and turned her toward the door. "We're finding other seats."

We took ourselves over to right field and easily found vacant seats where we watched the Guardians eek out a win over the Lancers. If it hadn't been for Joey, they would have lost for sure. If it hadn't been for Troy, they would have won without me having to leave bruises on Haley's arm from gripping it so hard.

I tried to push away my feelings about Brett and focus on Joey. There was only so much I could handle at once, and my emotions were all over the place. I didn't know what to do—as usual—so I settled for sending Brett a text during the seventh inning stretch.

Me: Hey there. Something came up, so we'll catch up later.

It was nice and vague. I was sure he had no clue his crazy goddess had waylaid me in the ladies and I wanted to keep it that way.

Brett: Where are you?

Well, he wasn't supposed to ask that. The last thing I needed was him coming to find us and Psycho Vergara pulling out her rusty pliers in the middle of Joey's game. So, I switched my phone off and shoved it back in my pocket.

Haley and I took Joey out for a late-night celebratory dinner after the game. He was running on an adrenaline high and it was so good to see him this excited. I had no doubt he'd be getting a call from his coach by the time the weekend was through.

We dropped him off close to midnight at his apartment, and like the good boy he is, he promised to hit the sack to rest up for tomorrow's game.

"Oh, man. I used to have such a crush on him back in college." Haley watched as Joey closed his apartment door behind him.

My mouth dropped open. "How did I not know that?"

She laughed. "It lasted for all of about two weeks before I realized I'd need a Master's degree in all things baseball to hold anything close to a painless conversation. He was cute, but not *that* cute."

I could only shake my head as I steered us toward my apartment. Why wouldn't you want to know all about baseball, regardless of a guy? "But if you guys got married, then we'd be officially related. You couldn't take one for the team?" I teased.

"Sorry, but I like my men a little more toward the cerebral side."

It was my turn to laugh. "Ha! You mean Professor Nerdboy."

Haley's face split in a wide grin and I could practically see her mind drifting away to thoughts of her cutie-pie neighbor. I was happy for her and keeping all my fingers and toes crossed that I wouldn't have to kill him for breaking her heart.

I sighed and turned into my complex. Haley jerked forward and out of her reverie when I slammed on the brakes.

Brett stood in front of my building, hands in his pockets, ass leaning against the wall, and eyes squinting as my headlights blinded him.

"What the hell?" Haley muttered before catching sight of Brett, upon which her voice changed to the same cooing tone she uses with dogs and babies. "Oooooohhhhh." I put a light foot to the accelerator again and eased into my parking spot. "I freaking love this guy."

I shushed her as I put the car in park and peered out my windshield at him. He pulled a hand from his pocket and sent us a hesitant wave. My heart started jackhammering.

Before I could stop her, Haley pulled my keys from the ignition, jumped out of the car, and slammed the door behind her. I opened my door to grab her or maybe kill her, but all I got was an, "I'll just be upstairs in the guest room! Hi, Brett!" before she disappeared up the stairs, leaving me alone with Brett in the dimly lit parking lot.

He pushed off the wall and ran a hand through his hair. "So, I guess you met Ari."

Assuming he meant the model with a toolbox full of rusty weapons, I extended a fake-ass half smile and nodded.

Brett shook his head and sighed. "Why didn't you answer your phone? I was worried."

He was worried? What, did this Ari chick get away from him and follow me? My eyes darted around the parking lot before I could regain a level head. I decided to play dumb, a.k.a. lie my ass off. "Oh, sorry. We were out celebrating and I must not have heard my phone."

"That's okay." He stepped closer, his shoes scuffing on the cement. "I wanted to see for myself that you were okay, and I need to apologize."

Ugh. Here it came. *Sorry, but my new woman doesn't want me hanging out with you.* I was grateful to have my open door as a barrier between us—and a support to keep me upright.

I waved a hand in front of me like I was being consumed by a swarm of giant mosquitos. "No, no, no. You don't need to apologize."

He gave a half laugh. "Why do I feel like we're always having this conversation?"

I smiled half-heartedly, because he wasn't wrong.

He took one more step and the light from the building caught the wayward flip of his hair where it was mussed from his hand. "And you *definitely* deserve an apology."

"Brett." I tilted my head. He didn't owe me a thing. I should be happy for him, and I'd get there. One day.

He continued as if I hadn't spoken, "But since Ari has been forbidden to come within 500 yards of you, I'm apologizing for her." My head jerked back at that, but he just continued. "I'm so sorry she came after you or threatened you or whatever. She got some crazy idea in her head and ran with it without checking her facts first. She's... impulsive."

I tried taking this all in, still not quite understanding what in the hell he was talking about. "But she likes you," was the only thing I could muster.

"Thank God. I'd hate to be on her shit list, that's for sure." He cringed, silently acknowledging that I was currently number one on that list. "Sorry."

Why had he come here? And what was he doing going out with someone he clearly thought was a bit nuts? Did he get off on that kind of thing? "It's okay. Really." I just wanted to go inside and be done with this conversation. There was a reality show, a bottle of wine, and my best friend waiting for me. I shut my door and rounded the front of my car, making a move for the building. I had to pass close by and I could smell his scent of sunscreen, grass, and soap. "No big deal, but thanks for the apology." I picked up my pace.

"Oh."

Thankfully, he didn't try to follow me. "She's very pretty, and I'm sure she has lots of good qualities." Like her ability to smother a man to death with her giant boobs.

"Uh, I guess."

"I gotta go." I threw a hand over my shoulder. "Talk later." And I sprinted up the stairs toward my door, not stopping until it was closed behind me. I panted, my back to the beveled surface, as my nose began to sting. No way. I was not going to cry. I forced a lungful of air in and then let it out slowly, willing my heart to stop racing. I'd almost accomplished it when a loud knock by my ear startled the shit out of me and I yelped.

"Liv! Open the door!"

Of course it was Brett, but for a moment there I'd actually been hoping it was a serial killer instead. I bit my lip and stilled. But it wasn't as if I could pretend I wasn't there so I gathered my wits and turned around. I let the door open just a crack, determined to send him away.

Brett had other ideas. He pushed the door open and stalked past me. When he turned back my way, he wore a scowl. "What am I missing here? You didn't even let me finish explaining what happened today."

He had some nerve busting into my apartment and yelling at me. I crossed my arms. "I don't really feel like hearing anything else you have to say, to be honest."

His eyes swept the apartment before zeroing in on me again. Where in the hell was Tambo? What good was a huge dog if he wasn't even going to stick his head out to threaten intruders. Oh, who was I kidding—the most he'd do was drool on a robber and sniff their crotch.

"I don't know why you're acting this way. I thought we had fun today, and I just stood outside your apartment for two hours waiting to apologize for Ari."

I swear, if he said her name one more time I was going to throw something at him. My inner green-eyed monster was revving for a fight. "Look, I'm trying not to be a bitch, which is why I need you to leave."

He shook his head and threw his arms out to the sides. "What did I do? Tell me what I did."

I growled—actually growled. "You didn't do anything." My fists clenched and my chest got tight as I felt the tears threaten again.

He reached behind him and pulled his phone out of his pocket. "Here." He held it out to me. "You want to call Ari and yell at her?"

That was it. The dam burst and my voice rose about a dozen decibels. "No! I don't want to talk to her! Why in God's name would I want to talk to a woman who not only threatened to rip my fingernails out but is dating the same guy *I* want to date?! That's not my idea of a good time! I'm not sure what you expect from me, but if you think you can flirt with me while you're dating someone else, you've got another thing coming. And I can guarantee your *Ari* won't stand for it either. So please go back to your boobalicious mental case and leave me alone! It's bad enough that I have to get over you, but now we can't even be friends, so can't you see why I want you to *Just. Go. Away*!?" By the time I was done I couldn't even see Brett. My vision was blurred by the tears that escaped and I swiped at them furiously. I was so worked up, I could probably have felled an elephant with little effort.

I felt a warm hand on my arm. A gentle hand. And his words registered a split second before his lips landed on mine. "Thank fuck."

Chapter Fifteen

GOING DOWN

RETT

The kiss lasted all of about five seconds before she pulled back and coldcocked me right on my cheekbone.

"Ow!" I cradled my face as Liv danced around shaking her hand out and cussing. "What the hell was that for?"

I'd hated seeing her cry and when she admitted she had feelings for me, I couldn't do anything but kiss her. Apparently, that hadn't been the smartest move.

"You kissed me!"

"Uh, yeah. And I plan to do it again once my face stops throbbing."

"You are unbelievable."

There were several jokes I could think of to respond with, but I didn't know that I could handle another punch so soon after the last one, even if it was from a tiny fist like Liv's. "You said you wanted to date me. I just assumed that would include kissing."

She rolled her eyes—eyes that were now clear of tears, I noted. "Are you brain damaged? Did we not just have an entire conversation about the other woman you're already dating?"

I bit my lip to keep from laughing. She was fucking cute when she was mad. She rubbed at her hand and growled at my expression, the second growl of the night by my count. It was time to clear up this clusterfuck.

But just as I opened my mouth to speak, the door to her apartment flew open and banged against the wall. Liv and I both turned to find fucking Horner with his arms propped on the door frame, his chest heaving, eyes wild and sweat beading on his forehead. Great. It's never a party until the giant Kool-Aid guy busts in.

"Liv," he panted, and I stepped in front of her before I could even think about it. It was like I was asking to be a human punching bag today.

"Seriously?" she asked.

There was no way this douchebag was taking one more step. "Horner, man, you need to go."

Liv stepped out from behind me and propped her hands on her hips, scowling at both of us. Her head swiveled as if she couldn't decide who to stab first. "You *both* need to go."

My "No way" and Troy's "We need to talk" overlapped and Liv's eyes continued to pinball. I curled my lip at Troy but he only had eyes for Liv. Why wasn't he going all caveman on me like all our previous encounters?

"Liv, we're not done talking. Not by a long shot," I interjected. She needed to understand that there was nothing between me and Ari—and a whole hell of a lot between me and her.

She wrinkled her nose at me and then made a strangled sound.

"Livvy, please." That came from Troy who, I had to give him credit, still hadn't crossed over the threshold.

Liv shot him an angry finger. "*Don't* call me that. You don't have the right."

He hung his head, still breathing heavily. And, was that a look of remorse on his face? The world was going crazy.

"What the hell are *you* doing here, asshole?" Our eyes all darted to the entrance to the living room where Haley stood flanked by Tambo and a small brown dog I'd never seen before. Her stance mirrored Liv's and, had Troy and I been wiser men, we probably would have hauled ass out of there.

Tambo trotted over and sat on my shoe. I tried not to wince.

"Really?" Liv eyed the dog, making me want to smile again, despite the tension crackling in the air.

Troy's strained voice cut through the room. "They're sending me back down."

Liv and I stilled. Even Tambo froze. Everyone was silent for a beat and then Haley broke in. "I'm sorry. What does that even mean, and why should Liv care, anyway? You cheated on her."

She did have a point.

But this was like when you prayed for the school bully to get explosive diarrhea in gym class and you find out the next day that he's been hit by a car and is stuck in a full-body cast all summer.

"Troy, I…" Liv trailed off, her voice suddenly quiet.

It was unclear to me whether Troy's careless behavior of late was the chicken or the egg in this scenario. Had he known this was coming? Either way, it signaled the likely end of any real baseball career for him.

Liv bit her lip and I couldn't even blame her when she looked to me and then Haley. "Would you guys mind taking the dogs out while I talk to Troy for a minute?"

Haley inhaled sharply, but I shot her a small shake of my head before nudging the giant dog to move off my foot. He groaned but complied when a scowling Haley approached with two leashes. Troy moved aside as we passed and she delivered some serious smack-talk using just her eyes.

"Don't close the door, Liv. We'll be downstairs so shout if you need us." Her gaze shifted to Liv. She gave her friend a long look and the side of Liv's mouth lifted in a half-hearted smile of appreciation.

"Well, that didn't go how I expected," Haley finally said to me when we hit the bottom of the stairs. She had both leashes in her hands and controlled the two dogs like it was second nature. "I figured the two of you would have worked your shit out and been mauling each other by now." She shot me a grin.

I grimaced in return. "That *had* been the plan."

She tipped her chin. "See, I knew you weren't dating anyone. I tried to tell her."

"Thanks for that. Now I just need to get Liv to believe it."

"Don't worry." Haley sent me a reassuring smile before glancing back up toward Liv's apartment. "What the hell was all that with Troy?"

I sighed, battling with the part of me that felt sorry for him. "He's getting a demotion to a lower farm team. It's pretty much the kiss of death at his level."

She just nodded again, giving me no clue to her thoughts on the matter. I couldn't exactly blame her for hating the guy like any self-respecting best friend would. I watched as the dogs sniffed around the narrow grassy area and we waited. "Haley?"

"Yeah," she answered absently.

"Did you know your dog is missing a leg?" I don't know how

it had taken me so long to notice—I guess I just figured it had been holding its leg up for some reason.

She smiled at me like I was an idiot she was being paid to befriend. "I might have noticed that, yes."

"Just checking."

She looked at me a moment longer. "Brett?"

"Yeah."

"What happened to your face?"

My hand came up to my tender cheek and I couldn't help the smile spreading on my face. I didn't even care that it made the ache worse. "I kissed her and she punched me."

Haley held her lips between her teeth, her eyes wide with shocked amusement. Then she gave up and burst out laughing.

Ten minutes later, Haley and I were both ready to bust up the little tête-à-tête upstairs. Visions of Liv in Troy's arms refused to vacate my mind, and I imagined every possible way in which he could work the situation to his advantage. I mean, Liv still thought I was dating Ari, for God's sake. Liv *had* to know she and I were supposed to be together!

So, when Troy slowly descended the stairs without Liv on his arm, I let out a relieved breath and stopped my pacing on the side-walk. Haley didn't hesitate to brush right past him and up the stairs with the dogs in tow like they were all rescuing Liv from a burning building.

Troy stopped a few feet from me and scrubbed both his hands over his short blond hair. He was wearing gym shorts and one of those sweat-wicking t-shirts that all these guys wore off the field. I didn't know what to say—or if I wanted to say anything at all. He'd treated Liv like crap and hurt her. But do you kick a dog when he's down? Even if he deserves it? Turned out I didn't have to decide.

"Just take care of her, okay?"

That was all he said before opening the door of a rusted-out pick-up and getting in. He was gone before I could even take a breath to tell him that hell would freeze over before I'd let anything bad happen to Olivia Sun.

When I got back upstairs, I found Liv and Haley huddled together on the couch, both still in their Guardians gear. I wanted to demand to know what had happened between Liv and Troy but, again, I didn't feel the need to see how her left hook compared to her right.

Haley caught my eye and sat up. "We'll talk more tomorrow. I don't know how much longer Brett can wait." Then she whispered something in Liv's ear and rose from the couch. "Come on, guys. You're bunking with me tonight," she beckoned the dogs who followed her with wagging tails. I heard the door shut at the end of the hall and then Liv and I were alone. Finally.

There was one thing I wanted to make clear. "I'm not leaving until we finish talking."

She put a hand up, not looking at me. "I don't know that I can handle any more talks tonight, Brett."

She sounded defeated and I hated that. Liv was bright and effervescent and sarcastic and joyful. My heart hurt at her tone. I dropped my shoulders and walked over to stand in front of her. "Hey." My voice was gentle, and she finally looked up and met my eyes. Hers were tense, a V etched between her brows.

Just when I thought she was going to freeze me out, she spoke. "Is it wrong that I feel bad for him?"

I drew in a slow breath and let out a mirthless laugh. "I was just asking myself the same question."

She spared me a tiny smile and I dropped down on the couch next to her. "The only reason I'm not kicking you out is because Haley made me promise not to." She tried to sound annoyed, but it didn't quite come off. "He's leaving tomorrow," she said after a minute. "They're sending him to Augusta, Georgia."

A small part of me railed that she sounded like she'd miss him, but I reined in my feelings before they could show. She was talking, so that was a good start. I'd always been her friend, and if that was what she needed right now, I'd have to put a hold on clearing the air between us until she worked her way through this Troy thing. But only for a little while.

"Did he say what reasons they gave?" *Besides acting like an insane moron tonight and being an overall asshole*, I added silently.

"They told him Double-A was for refinement, not development and he wasn't proving his maturity or discipline enough to stay." She chuffed. "None of us should be surprised about the maturity, I suppose." She turned to face me. "I asked him what the hell was up with him at the game tonight and he just said it was a long story. He was super vague, but he said something about just wanting to help and it all going wrong. He also promised to fix it." She ran a hand through her hair. "I have no idea what that means."

I froze mid-shrug. Ari's crazy story came rushing back.

I barely heard Liv when she continued talking. "I told him there was no possible way to fix things between us, but I didn't get the sense that that's what he was talking about."

I nodded absently. When Ari accused Liv of running a prescription drug business with Troy, I'd wanted to laugh. Liv was about as likely to be involved in that as she was to suddenly embrace ballet instead of baseball. But Troy... Troy was a wild card. And he was involved with at least one other woman we knew of, maybe more. Shit.

"Uh, Liv? I know this may sound like a strange question, but is there any reason to believe Troy could be mixed up with prescription drugs? Either abusing them or selling them… or both?"

She gave me a wary look and sat up straight on the couch. "Why?"

The fact that she hadn't outright dismissed the idea didn't say good things. I scratched my forehead, not sure how much I wanted to share at this point. I mean, I'd been ready to tell her the whole damn story to explain away Ari's crazy behavior and ridiculous threat, but I'd thought it was just that. Ridiculous. Now I wasn't so sure.

"Do you think he's on something? Is that why he was so odd at the game and so worked up when he came here?" She bit her thumbnail and studied my face.

I put my hands out. "Look, I have no real idea, and I don't know how much credence I'd give to a third-hand account of a conversation in a women's restroom." She blinked at me and I hurried on. "One of my friends was in the women's room at the stadium and heard some girls talking about a small-time prescription drug business Troy and a girlfriend were supposedly running." I purposely didn't mention Ari's name. I could explain all that later.

She shook her head, not focusing on me. "I mean, he's been icing his shoulder a bit and I caught him wincing several times, but I never saw any pain meds." She bit her lip again and met my gaze. "And, anyway, the team doctor would be all over it if Troy had an exemption filed to take any meds."

I shrugged. "Well, there goes that theory."

Liv stood up from the couch then. "God, I hope it's nothing big. I don't know that I can handle Troy trying to 'fix' anything."

Again, I wanted to ask exactly what he'd said, where they'd talked, whether he'd laid a hand on her—but I knew I couldn't. It wasn't my right. She walked toward the entryway to her apartment and I could tell she expected me to follow.

"At least he apologized for cheating on me and then stalking me like an asshole. Not that I needed him to—I wrote him off weeks ago. But 'I'm sorry' is always good to hear anyway." Her voice started to trail off and she turned, obviously assuming I'd be right behind her.

I wasn't. With my ass firmly planted on her couch, I took a deep breath. "Well, I'm glad you think so, because I'm sorry too."

She put a staying hand out and her mouth turned down. "Brett…"

But I cut her off. "I'm sorry, but I'm not leaving until we talk some more about you wanting to date me." I quirked a brow and would not have blamed her one bit for coldcocking me again.

Chapter Sixteen

LET'S GET PHYSICAL

IV

My cheeks caught fire and I couldn't tell if it was from embarrassment or anger. What was it with these guys demanding I talk to them right when it suited them? What if I didn't want to talk? I blamed the shocking news of Troy being sent down to a High-A farm team for my allowing him to stay and talk. And that little conversation had brought up more questions than it had answered. I wasn't going to let Brett shoulder his way into a heart-to-heart. I'd already blurted out that I had a thing for him—I didn't need to hear all about how he could fit me into his rotation or whatever. Gah! I feared the feelings I had for him weren't the kind I could keep casual. Not to mention one of his harem wanted to assassinate me.

I was just about to tell him exactly where he could stick his "I'm sorry" when he beat me to the punch.

"I do not now, nor will I ever, date Ari Amante. That girl is batshit crazy." He finally drew himself up to standing as I froze on my tile floor. "In my opinion, she is one poor decision away from an O.J.-style car chase, complete with wailing sirens and news helicopter coverage." He took a step closer and my heart picked up its pace as his words began to sink in. "I mean, she should come with a warning label for any guy who even contemplates going there. You don't even want to know what she did to her latest ex-boyfriend." A visible shudder ran through his body and he paused his slow steps, meeting my eyes. His voice quieted. "She's Emerson's best friend. That's it."

My mouth dropped open and I felt my brows drawing together. When I finally regained the ability to form words, they didn't work quite how they were supposed to. "But. What. I. That. You. She. What." I closed my mouth and breathed in through my nose, no longer able to focus on Brett, but instead choosing a patch of blue wall behind him.

"What I didn't get a chance to explain before was that Ari was the one who overheard the conversation in the women's room. She got it in her head that the girlfriend was you and, in some weirdly overprotective impulse, decided to get in your face. I already set her straight about you, so you don't need to worry about Ari. In fact, I wouldn't be surprised if she tracked you down to apologize—even though I told her she's done enough already. She may be crazy, but her heart's in the right place. At least I think it is."

My eyes finally swung back to Brett and I saw he had his hands shoved in his front pockets again. I didn't want to think how much I adored that little habit of his. I was still processing the Ari thing, but I couldn't stop myself from asking, "Then who *are* you dating?"

His brow furrowed until he resembled a wrinkled Shar-Pei puppy. "You?" I could see him holding his breath. Dammit.

I let out a frustrated huff at his intentional obtuseness. "You had a date just last weekend."

He stared blankly at me, making me want to punch him, kiss him, and roll my eyes at him. "At Lindley Park Filling Station. With Ginger, maybe?" How could he not remember this? Perhaps Troy wasn't the one on drugs here.

His head pulled back and he continued the blank stare until, all at once, his face brightened as if a light had just been switched on. "That was for Jay, not me! Remember Emerson's little brother, the pitcher? He was going on his first date and asked me where to take the girl." Then he frowned and shook his head. "And for the record, there's no way in hell I'm dating Ginger."

I digested this new information, knowing my emotions plastered themselves across my face one after another as I comprehended what this meant. He wasn't dating Ari. He wasn't dating Ginger. He wasn't dating anyone. Except… me. My eyes shot to his face as a clawing horror swept over me. "I punched you!"

Brett just rubbed his cheek and grinned—I punched him and the guy grinned! "You did."

I covered my mouth with both hands. "Oh my God." And then my feet were moving and I was coming at him. I barreled into Brett, sending him back on a foot as I threw my arms around him and buried my head in his shirt. "I'm so sorry. I'm so, so sorry." I inhaled his familiar scent and held on tight.

His arms met at my back. "Don't worry about it. It's not the first time I've been punched. In fact, it's not even the first time I've been punched this month." I groaned at his terrible joke and hugged him even harder. He may have grunted, but I figured if I ruptured one of his kidneys I had an extra one he could have.

I finally pulled back to look up at him again and his hands came around to cup my face. His lips were tipped up and his blue eyes shone bright as they scanned my face. I bit my bottom lip and knew my face had to be a mess from the day outside and all the emotion of the last few hours. But that wasn't what I saw reflected in his eyes as he watched me. I got the distinct impression he was about to kiss me, but apparently he wasn't done messing with me just yet.

"You've got a decent arm. Ever thought about playing ball?"

My lips formed a reluctant smile and I couldn't seem to muster up a reply. Which was okay because that was when he leaned in and placed the softest kiss on my lips. It was like a sigh, a long exhale after a harrowing day, a settling in when you finally return home. I felt it all in his tender kiss.

I took his upper lip between mine and felt his beard and mustache brush over my skin as we engaged in this exquisitely unhurried kiss. Our heads slanted effortlessly, and he took a small taste of my lip with his tongue while I brought a hand up to stroke the overly long hair at his nape.

The kiss was slow, an intimate act unto itself—one that wasn't a prelude to anything else, but a savoring of that very moment in time and the connection we'd been denying between us—the connection I still didn't understand. This kiss was a confession, and it was such a relief to be able to unburden myself as our mouths lazily worshipped one another.

It sent a smoldering burn down to my belly and it kept creeping lower until the flickers turned into a roaring fire, searing this man into the very core of me. He was everywhere inside me—my chest, my gut, my head, and I liked him exactly where he was.

But as much as I loved this kiss and everything it meant, my body began to beg for more. So it wasn't all that surprising when I noticed my hand had wandered to the vicinity of the pronounced bulge in his jeans. One minute, I was stroking his hair and shoulders and the next I was totally copping a feel. I couldn't feel bad about it and didn't even try, instead giving him a squeeze through his jeans. He groaned into my mouth and his hips twitched forward.

I grinned against his mouth and pulled away, not missing the near pout on his face at my movement.

"Come with me." I pulled him by the hand toward my bedroom down the short hall. A glance over my shoulder revealed his hungry focus on my ass as his tongue traced a path over his lower lip. This was so on. He looked close to outright pouncing on me when I shut the door behind me and immediately peeled off my Guardians shirt. I didn't need to look down to know he had a clear view of my hardened nipples beneath the almost sheer fabric of my white lace bra. My spine tingled when he hurriedly closed the distance between us, his eyes practically ablaze.

"Wow." I smiled and threaded my fingers together behind his neck. "That's an intense look you've got going there."

His jaw was literally ticking with what I assumed was the restraint he was attempting to exercise, and when he only grunted in return, I couldn't help but laugh. He didn't even seem to notice as all his focus homed in on the spot where his thumbs ran over my nipples. I sucked in a breath at the sensation. It was only moments until the lace cups fell away, revealing my naked breasts to his gaze. I didn't have even a second to bemoan the small size of them before Brett bent and covered one with his mouth while his hand cupped the other one. His inhale was audible when he swirled his tongue around my tight bud. It was so erotic and intense, I moaned and held the back of his head in case he had any crazy ideas of moving from that exact spot. I didn't need to worry, it turned out.

But, as with all things, I couldn't abide him pulling too far ahead of me for too long. To that end, my hands drifted down and peeled up his black t-shirt, necessitating the departure of his lips from my breasts. Then we were skin on skin for the first time and it was fantastic. I felt the goosebumps rise on my stomach and arms as I smoothed my hands over the warm, firmness of his shoulders.

"Jesus, Brett." I pulled back for a couple seconds, looking him over. His clothing did a good job of hiding the lovely treat that lingered beneath. Well-defined muscles lined his arms, shoulders, chest, and stomach and I felt my mouth water for a taste. "You're kind of cut."

He laughed at my outburst and it was possible his chest swelled a tad at my words. I thought back to the night at his apartment when I'd gotten my first glimpse of his torso, but I'd been so focused on his injuries and the guilt over Troy that I guess I'd gone into clinical mode and the leanly-muscled goodness hadn't registered. Dr. Sun was out of the office tonight, though, that was for damn sure. I feathered my fingers over his taut stomach where his laughter tightened the muscles. "Nice." I glanced up with what I knew was a saucy grin and then bent to run my tongue over the skin above his navel. The laughter died in his throat and his entire body stiffened as I continued my exploration and inhaled his masculine scent.

I'd hardly gotten started, though, when Brett pulled me upright and ran his hands over my shoulders until I looked up at him again. I knew my eyes were lust drunk, and his were in agreement, but he was studying me again with that hot gaze. I felt my insides go all tingly and my sex clench.

"Come here," he coaxed with a quiet tone, and pulled me to the bed. Now we were talking! If I thought this was the first step in the fast track to get-me-some town, however, I was sorely mistaken. He lay down on my soft gray sheets and pulled me down next to him so we were facing each other. My confusion must have been written on my face because he brought a finger up to smooth the skin between my brows. What was happening here?

"God, you're so beautiful."

He spoke with such earnestness that I almost panicked at my sudden inability to process his words. I felt the color rise to my cheeks, and it didn't escape me how backward it was that a heart-felt compliment could embarrass me while running my tongue down this man's happy trail didn't merit even a touch of self-consciousness. Not knowing what to do with myself, I leaned forward for a kiss. But Brett pulled away after a brief touch of our lips. I fought a protest.

His thumb circled the skin of my bare shoulder. "Hey, I just want to make sure we're not moving too fast here."

He could have knocked me over with a feather. Too fast? It was clear we were both into each other, we knew we got along, we always had a good time. Troy was completely out of the picture and Brett wasn't dating anyone else. I looked pointedly down at my naked boobs before meeting his gaze again.

"Uh, I'm good. You?"

When he didn't answer right way, I leaned in again. It was nice and all of him to be a gentleman about the whole thing, but I was most certainly good to go—the sooner the better if the state of my panties was anything to go by. But he held me back by that hand on my shoulder again.

"Believe me, I can't wait to get you naked and be inside you."

Well, thank goodness for that! I was starting to think I'd stumbled into one of those alternate universes where the crazy advanced humans had dispensed with sex entirely in favor of bizarre scientific procreation inside a sterile petri dish. I mean, what was the fun in that?

He removed his hand from my shoulder and used it to stroke his beard. This was not helping, as it only brought to mind how that beard would feel against certain areas of my body. "I just... I just don't want this to be all about sex." He put his hand up. "I know. I'm just as surprised as you."

His attempt at levity made one corner of my mouth quirk and then I felt my face turned sort of soft. He was treating me—treating *us*—with such care it caused a lump to form in my throat. This was such uncharted territory for me, I was in need of a very *very* detailed map as soon as humanly possible. And perhaps a sedative for my nerves, now that I thought about it.

My hand came up and I pressed my palm to his cheek. He turned and kissed it and I tried to swallow before speaking what was swirling around in my heart and gut. "It's not." I shook my head and saw him watching me carefully. "I've never been very good at this part, but I want to be good at it with you." And it was true. Sex was easy. Intimacy was harder.

He nodded and I could see relief carved in his features. "It's okay to get freaked out, Liv, but you have to promise to tell me if you do."

I nodded my agreement, not sure that I could speak just then. I would do my very best and I'd have to hope it would be enough. When he leaned forward and pressed a gentle kiss to my forehead, though, I felt it register right in my heart—that stubborn organ that didn't get as much use as it probably should.

It wasn't that I'd made any conscious decision to avoid intimacy or deeper feelings with a man, and it's cliché to say, but I'd been freaking busy. Veterinary school is no joke. Physicians have to learn how one body—the human body—functions. Vets need to learn how hundreds do and how to diagnose problems when their patients can't describe their symptoms with words. When your focus is on one very taxing endeavor, it doesn't leave time for more than casual relationships. And I happen to love sex, so it was sort of a no-brainer. This thing with Brett—the unfamiliar depth of emotions—was entirely new. And, I'm not going to lie, it was scary as shit. But I knew down to my bones that I'd regret not trying. I just had to hope neither of our hearts would break.

So, with my heart thumping a heavy beat, I took a deep breath and said the words. "I promise." The smile I got in return did amazing things to not just my nerves, but my inexperienced heart.

"Oh my God," I moaned as I met Brett's eyes and my tongue came out to sweep over my bottom lip. The swelling of his pupils didn't go unnoticed as he watched my mouth while I slowly slid the fork out. "You weren't kidding about this pie," I mumbled over my mouthful of utterly delectable chocolate pecan pie. One of his friends had a catering business and had given him a cooler bag that day with a pie in it—something about a single guy needing someone to feed him. I'd let that woman move into my apartment and feed Brett if it meant I could get in on more goodies like this. Best. Pie. Ever.

Brett still hadn't taken a bite of his, I noticed. He seemed too busy studying my mouth, a notion that made me feel all hot again. But after our talk in the bedroom, I hadn't protested when he suggested we get dressed and take a little breather before we lost our heads and banged the hell out of each other. Well, those weren't his exact words, but it captures the gist of it. He was treating this beginning between us as a fragile thing to be protected and cherished, and who was I to dismiss such a thoughtful intention? This man kept showing me more and more layers and taking this step back forced me to acknowledge it all and not shove it under the bed while we wrecked the sheets.

So pie it was. Damn spectacular pie at that.

But, while one part of Brett approved of this take-it-slow plan, the other parts were obviously not in complete agreement. As was proved when he bolted out of his chair and moved to the fridge, the bulge in his jeans quite apparent. I snickered to myself and forked another bite of pie.

"Do you have any water?"

I grinned unabashedly. "There might be a couple bottles in the fridge, but if not, just take some from the tap. It's safe." I didn't know why I always added that last part except for all that stuff with my mom.

My grin began to die and I felt my face fall. I could hear Brett grumbling something as he pulled a glass from the cabinet. But our conversation from earlier came rushing back and I couldn't ignore it once it was stuck in my mind.

I set my fork down. "Brett?"

He turned from the counter, empty glass in hand. "Yeah." When he saw my expression he came closer. "What's the matter?"

I was lightheaded, but I pushed on. "Earlier tonight. When you talked about that prescription drug business and Troy with some girl."

Brett sat back down at the table and I blinked at him. He returned my look with a questioning one. Not that I blamed him in light of my abrupt change in conversation.

I stood from the table, pie forgotten, and paced a couple times across the tile floor as I gathered my thoughts. Something wasn't right.

I'd been asking myself over and over why Troy kept pestering me when he was obviously getting sex elsewhere. It wasn't like he was in love with me. And then those looks he'd been sending me at the game and his desperate appearance at my door. Not to mention the ominous "I'll fix it" declaration.

"Do we have any idea who this girlfriend is?"

Brett shook his head and scratched his beard as he thought. "Not to bring up a sore subject, but I guess it could have been the girl I saw him with at Fever a few weeks ago. Tall brunette? Long hair?"

It didn't ring any bells, but that wasn't surprising. Brett set his glass down on the table and then it hit me. "Oh my God."

He stilled. "What?"

"He came to my office."

"*Who* came to your office?" Brett straightened, going on high alert. Even with this new revelation, I kind of melted a little at his protectiveness.

I took my thumbnail between my teeth and force myself to concentrate. Yes. This made sense. And it was not good.

"Troy. He came to my office a few times since we broke up. I thought he was trying to get back together, and I even had to call Joey on one occasion to get him to leave."

"Well, not that I understand most of the choices Troy makes, but I can see him wanting to get back together."

I resumed my pacing as I pulled at a strand of my hair. "But he had a much better chance of getting me in private coming here to the apartment. He specifically tried to get into my *office*." My eyes met Brett's for a long moment.

He released a breath and steepled his hands in front of him as his mouth turned down. "Where you keep medications, I gather?"

"It's worse." I finally walked back to the table and dropped down in my chair in defeat.

"I keep meticulous records of every medication I stock—and they're all in a locked cabinet."

"So he stole your keys?"

"No. He didn't need to." I swallowed. "God, I hope I'm wrong about this." I looked back at Brett and he reached out to squeeze my hand where it worried the wood of the tabletop. "I've been collecting expired and unused medications from clients so I can drop them off at the hospital for proper disposal. My mom... well, it's complicated."

He nodded, not needing all the details but listening attentively regardless.

"Anyway, I've been keeping them in a tox container in my office until I know I'll be driving by the hospital. My office is always locked when I'm not there."

He nodded, knowing exactly where I was going with this. "Except when your boyfriend drops by."

I nodded back. "Troy would sometimes stop by my work and I'd leave him in the office while I went to the bathroom or greeted a client."

"Leaving him the opportunity to cherry pick the best drugs and leave the rest so you wouldn't notice."

"Exactly." I ran my hands over my face. "But, Brett, not only are a lot of these drugs expired, they're not up to the same FDA standards as medications intended for humans."

"Shit."

"Yeah, shit is right. And I don't have complete records of everything I've collected over these past few months."

Brett took a breath and sat back in his chair, his pie still untouched in front of him. "This is all speculation, though, right? Maybe he never took anything. I mean, why would a guy with a baseball career risk losing it all to make a few random drug sales? It's more probable he was just going crazy without you."

I leaned forward on an elbow. "It's kind of sweet of you to say that, as weird as this is, but has Troy been acting like a guy who makes good decisions to you?"

Brett bit his lip and his eyebrows went up. "Uh, no." He pulled at one of the plugs in his earlobe. "So, what are we going to do?"

I looked at the clock and saw it was after one in the morning. "Nothing tonight, but tomorrow's another story."

He leaned forward and took my hand in his again, stroking my wrist with his thumb. Despite the unsettling discovery we'd made, I felt a shiver run over me. "Well, then I guess we may as well finish our pie."

The part of me that hoped that was a euphemism whimpered, but I managed to polish off my slice regardless before snuggling up with Brett in my bed for a very adult sleepover. My first one.

Chapter Seventeen

PERFECTLY INSANE AND INSANELY PERFECT

RETT

I woke to my dick screaming at me. Not that I blamed him after what I'd put him through over the last twelve hours, but let's just say he was making his opinion known. I tried to subtly adjust myself, however, he wouldn't be deterred.

"The promise land is within reach and it will be mine, fuck you very much, MacKinnon!" he hollered as my hips took over and my hard-as-rock cock homed in on the warmth between Liv's thighs, grinding into her very fine backside where it happened to be nestled right up to me in her bed.

One hand rested on her hip and I felt her stir in front of me as I tried to regain control. The struggle was a fierce one. She'd given me the green light last night and I could have been buried balls deep in her sweet, hot center for the better part of the night. But, no. My mind and heart decided to overrule my cock. I don't know who was more surprised, me or Liv.

It had just seemed so... crucial at the time. And it wasn't that I didn't trust Liv. I knew now that she'd never intentionally use me for sex—a notion that, at any other time in my life, I would have found laughable—but I didn't know if she trusted herself to not cut and run if things got too intense. My feelings for her were complicated as hell and I didn't get the sense she'd done complicated before.

So I was trying to keep things from getting too out of control too fast—since I was relatively certain that the minute I got a real taste of Liv, I'd be holed up in a bedroom with her for a good month or so. And if she decided she wasn't ready for something real at that point, I don't know that I'd be able to bounce back. Ever.

With that in mind, I took a quiet inhale to get my fix of that faint citrus scent she must use on her hair or skin and gently rolled myself to my back. I saw Liv's body move in my peripheral vision and I froze. It was no use. She rolled over, eyes sleepy and a naughty as hell grin on her lips.

"Good morning to you too." Her hair was a rumpled mess and she looked like she'd been freshly fucked. My cock stood at attention, hurling more insults at me. Liv didn't miss the movement under the sheets. How could she, really? The damn thing was forming a tent big enough to fit her huge dog.

"Oh my. Now what do we have here?" She made a move to lift the sheet and I slammed my hand down on the covers.

She pouted like a five-year-old—a horny five year old. Which was all kinds of wrong. "Party pooper."

"This is strictly a party for one." I narrowed my eyes at her when she wouldn't stop grinning.

Then she went up on her elbow, extending one hand to draw circles on my bare chest with a fingertip. I was only wearing boxer briefs and she was in another set of those miniscule excuses for pajamas. We'd talked in bed until we fell asleep the night before and I hadn't really considered how we might curl into each other in our sleep. So there I was with painful morning wood and a wicked siren tempting me first thing.

"It's not technically a party if there's only one person partici-pating, you know." Her hand dipped a bit lower until it encoun-tered the edge of the sheet that was doing a piss poor job at protecting my modesty. Damn, but she looked like a dream with that gorgeous smile and her hair creating a dark halo around her face. And I was only human.

"Fuck it," I said a half second before I claimed her mouth and pulled her over me.

She squealed and laughed into my mouth as she kissed me right back and got comfortable on top of me. Feeling her weight settle just right was pure heaven, and it only got better as she spread her thighs and nestled her hot core over my aching cock.

My hands dipped low to grab her asscheeks, and I used my fingers to trace the edge of her tiny shorts. She delved her tongue in my mouth just as I slid one finger under the hem to find the silky smooth heat hiding under.

"Oh, God," she moaned as she ground on me, sending dots of black through my vision. If I wasn't careful, I was going to embar-rass myself in no time.

But that possibility proved moot when there was a sharp series of knocks on Liv's bedroom door.

Liv let out a pained noise and straightened. "I'll give you a hundred dollars to come back later!" she yelled over her shoulder.

Haley's muffled voice sounded through the door. "I'm so sorry,

Livvy, but your security company just called your phone. Your office alarm is going off!"

"I keep telling you, I didn't leave my keys in the lock." Liv ran her hand through her hair for the tenth time since we'd arrived.

The police officer standing with her sighed and tried again. "Miss, people do it all the time. You were probably just distracted." She shook her head. "Or you were talking on the phone." He raised a condescending eyebrow. Her expression sharpened as she took a step toward him and I figured it might be a good time to intervene.

I quickly stepped up, giving a short shake of my head to tell her she should wipe the scowl off her face and probably refrain from assaulting an officer of the law. Not that she took any notice.

"Do I look stup—" And that was my cue to cut her off.

"Hello, Officer." I extended my hand with a polite smile. "Brett MacKinnon. The boyfriend," I announced myself, feeling Liv's scowl transfer to me. The officer, an older guy with salt-and-pepper hair and a slow gait who was probably nearing retirement age and definitely nearing his lunch break, looked me over and appeared less than impressed. But I pushed on. Somebody had to save Liv from herself. "I think what *Dr.* Sun was about to suggest was that she take a look around to make sure nothing is missing." I was sure to put the emphasis on the doctor part, figuring an old-school guy like this might be more inclined to give her a modicum of respect if she had a fancy title in her name. I could guess exactly what he thought of *me* as I stood in yesterday's clothes with my tangled mop and unkempt facial hair.

He looked between us and I tried to make up for the frown I

knew Liv was wearing by maintaining my polite smile. He finally nodded. "Fine. My partner and I already checked and there's nobody inside. And, like I said, no sign of forced entry." He gave Liv a pointed look. This was information he'd imparted twice now, along with his theory that Liv left her office keys in the front door where the wind must have rattled them and set off the alarm.

Needless to say, Liv was spitting mad, and they had yet to let her inside. We didn't need to speak to one another to know exactly where she'd be looking first upon entry.

The other officer, who'd remained silent for the most part, opened the door and gestured for Liv and me to go through. He held the keys out to Liv and she took them with a nod.

"Thank you, Officer," She said pointedly, turning around to pin the older guy with her glare. I just shook my head and put my hands on her shoulders from behind. You know, in case she decided to go all ninja on me.

As I knew she would, Liv headed straight for her private office before quickly unlocking the door to let us both in. My eyes darted around the unfamiliar space. Her gaze went straight for a rectangular red container in the corner of the room. A plastic grocery bag sat on top of it and Liv strode toward it with purpose. I stood back, waiting for her reaction to whatever lay inside.

"Well, holy shit."

Her eyes turned to me and she shook the bag, the unmistakable sound of pills rattling in their bottles ringing through the room. I finally approached and we both peered into the bag. Liv brought it over to her desk and began pulling out bottle after bottle, inspecting their labels and making various humming sounds at each one. Once they were all lined up, she propped her hands on her hips and took in the display.

"What do you want to do?"

She took a deep breath and let it out slowly as she peered in the direction of the front of the building where Officer Lunchbreak was undoubtedly waiting for us to hurry the hell up so he could get out of there.

"Idiot," she finally mumbled with a shake of her head. It was unclear if she was talking about Troy or the cop. It probably applied in either case. With one final huff, she quickly shoved all the bottles back in the bag and put the whole thing inside the red container before shutting the lid and turning to me. She shrugged and I caught her lower lip trembling.

That was enough. I walked over and pulled her into my arms, rubbing her back as she took shuddering breaths against my chest. I understood. I really did. This was a situation where there was no clear-cut decision she could feel good about. We had very little evidence pointing to Troy. We had no clue who the girlfriend was. There was no way to know how many bottles or pills were missing. And, most glaring of all, there was Troy's face as he stood at the threshold of Liv's apartment, his life falling apart at the seams as he finally acknowledged it was all imploding. Although the clear fact that he'd swiped her keys during the visit surely irked her.

When she got ahold of herself again, she scanned the large glass cabinet on the other side of the office that also held various medications. She seemed satisfied that it hadn't been tampered with and we walked together to the front of the building. This time without the snark. She locked the front door as I stepped forward.

"Everything's in order," I said so Liv wouldn't have to. She shot me a grateful look as she approached and I reached out for her hand.

The older cop let out a put-upon sigh and held out some paperwork to Liv. "Sign here." He pointed and handed her the paper and a pen. His partner walked by with a nod as Liv silently signed her name and handed everything back over. I moved to shake hands with the officer but he just turned without a word and fell in step next to his partner.

"You'd think a doctor would be smart enough to date a guy with a job—or at least a razor and a bar of soap." Officer Lunchbreak didn't even try to keep his voice down as the two cops walked to their patrol car and he snickered at his own joke.

The words had barely registered in my brain when Liv's hand broke free from mine and she was striding their way like a hockey player who'd just been head checked from behind and was looking for a fight.

Shit.

"Where do you get off throwing around insults like that?!" She pointed blindly back to me with a forceful finger. "You don't know him. You don't know a single thing about him!"

I hurried forward and put a hand on her shoulder just as the younger cop did the same to his partner when he turned back around—smug smile in place. We were both shaken off.

"Liv, it's not worth it," I hissed at her, praying she'd just let it go.

But she shot me a look, her brown eyes blazing into mine. "Yes, it is." She swung her head to face the cop again as he pinned her with a steely-eyed glare.

"You'd better watch your tone, missy, or you're gonna find yourself with more trouble than you bargained for."

"Marv." His partner gave a low warning, which he ignored.

"And if you're so sure somebody else left your keys in the door, take a look behind you. I'd say your culprit is right there."

That was definitely the wrong thing to say. Liv gasped, one hand hitting her hip and the other pointing an angry finger at the jerk. "That *guy*—the one with the beard and the hair and the sloppy t-shirt—is smarter than you'll ever hope to be! And, not only that, he's kind and generous and funny. He's open-minded and non-judgmental—unlike *some* people." She pulled in a breath, and drew herself up to her fullest height, which happened to be a pretty unimpressive five-foot-three at best. "*And* he has a great job, I'll have you know! He's the best man I know and he's perfect just the way he is!" Her voice dropped off a bit as she continued. "Apart from being a little too good at pool and maybe bowling, but whatever."

She was starting to lose her focus and a bit of her fire, but I was already smiling by this point.

The older cop maintained his sneer, but his partner had succeeded in prodding him along to the patrol car.

But, of course, Liv wasn't done. And her voice had regained its fervor.

"In fact, he's so thoughtful we haven't even had sex yet! He wants to wait until he's sure I'm all in. How's *that* for a stand-up guy?! Huh? Any woman would be lucky to have him as her boyfriend!"

Her audience had already reached their car and gotten in, leaving just me as the sole witness to her utter insanity. And it was perfect. Perfectly insane, yes. But also just perfect.

I slowly moved to stand in front of her and put both hands on her shoulders, knowing I wore a stupid grin and not caring one bit.

I raised my eyebrows. "Wow."

Her gaze finally left the departing car and swung up to me, her fierce scowl still in place until my grin registered and she blinked.

"Just. Fucking. Wow."

She exhaled and dropped her hands to her sides, her body

finally relaxing. Her nose wrinkled, making me want to haul her up and kiss the hell out of her.

"Some people are so stupid, you know?" She peered up at me.

I nodded a little too long, enjoying the shit out of watching her face. She'd gone to bat for me—completely unnecessarily, of course—but it still felt damn incredible. I gave it another few seconds before temptation got the best of me. "So, best man you know, huh?"

That turned her mouth down. "I've reconsidered my stance on that."

I shook my head. "Too late. It's already out there."

Her eyes narrowed. "And you can forget about any of that all-in stuff. Ever." She turned abruptly and my hands fell from her shoulders. My smile, however, stayed perfectly in place.

"You're just punishing both of us now, Liv!" I called after her as she stalked her pert little ass to my car. I followed and she was already in the passenger seat by the time I got there. I opened my door and sat down, in no particular hurry. When I turned to face her I could tell she was having a hard time holding up all her false indignation.

"Hey, Liv."

She made sure to pause for a few seconds before eventually turning to me with a beleaguered expression, weak though it was. "What."

I finally managed to school my expression. "You're perfect just the way you are too."

She opened her mouth, probably having expected me to say something different—something of the smart-ass variety. Then she shut it again.

I didn't miss the secret smile that curved her lips when she faced the windshield again and said, "Let's get out of here."

Chapter Eighteen

ARE YOU THERE, GOD? IT'S ME, OLIVIA

IV

That man was infuriating. And irresistible at the same time. So it was no surprise that I wanted to both strangle and kiss him following my bizarre outburst in the parking lot of my office. Thank God it was Sunday and nobody else was around to witness me completely losing my ever-loving shit and yelling at an officer of the law—about my sex life, no less. I had no idea what came over me, except that when I heard that asswipe talking shit about Brett my body and mouth had gone on autopilot. Unfortunately, my autopilot had been programed by a belligerent drunk.

Brett steered his car onto Benjamin Parkway and I could swear he was humming to himself. And then there was that faint grin with not a small degree of smugness to it. Good God. I was never going to live down the whole *best man I know* thing. Although his comment when he got in the car was pretty damn sweet, I had to admit. I'd never done sweet before, and I was thinking maybe I liked it. A little.

But I wasn't going to let myself melt into a puddle of goo in the passenger seat so, instead, I called Haley to fill her in. She'd stayed at the apartment because it made me nervous to leave it empty when someone may have just broken into my office. Clearly I'd seen too many *Law & Order* episodes. Or maybe just enough.

"I've been texting you for like a half hour, woman!" This was her greeting.

I gave her the rundown, including everything Brett and I had pieced together about Troy the night before and she was understandably pissed on my behalf. It was all part of the best friend gig.

"I can't believe the cops didn't even dust for prints or canvass the area for witnesses. Or look for nearby ATM camera footage that might have caught something." Haley had obviously seen her fair share of *Law & Order* as well.

"There was nothing missing, Hales. And the bastard cop wouldn't have believed anything I said anyway."

That was when Brett decided to be super helpful and chimed in with, "Except for the part about me being an awesome pool player. He believed that for sure."

I shoved his arm and pointed at the road while I switched my phone to the other ear.

"What does that mean?" Haley asked.

"Nothing. Brett forgot to take his meds this morning." He snickered and I stuck my tongue out at him.

"Sooooo." Her voice got all sing-songy and I covered my eyes with my free hand and braced. "You two seem pretty cozy. Can I assume you figured out he only has eyes for you, Dr. Sun?"

It was no use. I was going to spill everything to her anyway at some point. "I guess you could say that."

"And did you do the smart thing or the stupid thing?"

I felt my brows draw together and then shot a surreptitious glance Brett's way before facing the passenger side window and cupping a hand over the phone. "I can't talk about that right now," I mumbled quietly.

"Can't talk about what? It's a this-or-that question."

Another glance at Brett showed him only paying attention to the road ahead. I got back in position.

"Condoms. Sex. Being smart," I whispered.

"What? I can't hear you."

I nearly jumped out of my seat when Brett's voice boomed right next to my ear. "She's talking about sex. She told the officer about that too."

"Oh, for God's sake!" I was going to nut punch him as soon as he wasn't holding my life in his hands behind the wheel.

Haley and Brett both laughed.

"I don't know if I want to know that part of the story, Liv. I meant did you do the smart thing and tell him how you feel?"

"Oh."

I didn't say anything more right away, both because Brett was still eavesdropping like a high-school chick and because I wasn't sure how to answer. I mean, I'd told him I wanted to date him and that I wanted to open myself up to the idea of something deeper than just sex. And that didn't even account for all the crap I yelled in the parking lot. I didn't know if that covered the whole *how I feel* topic, but it said a lot if you asked me.

Again, though, I needed a map or rule book of some kind. Was it possible—or expected—to just make a decision to let someone into the deepest cracks and crevices of yourself? Wasn't that something that would happen naturally if it was supposed to? I didn't possess any kind of lock and key that I knew of—one I could hand over to Brett and say, "Hey, come on in and have a look around. *Mi casa es su casa.*" Although he'd probably appreciate the Spanish, come to think of it.

If I thought about it, I guess the best way to describe how I felt was… open to possibilities. That was pretty good, right? I peeked over at Brett as he got off on my exit. His long fingers gripped the steering wheel and when he flexed them, it made my nipples hard at the memory of those fingers on my skin. We came to a stop at the bottom of the ramp and I let my eyes travel up his arms to his neck where I'd kissed the warm spot behind his ear just this morning. He needed a shave and a trim of his beard, but I found myself thinking I wouldn't care if he just let the damn thing grow wild like a wooly beast. My lips turned up and, as if sensing it, Brett glanced my way and did a double take. His eyes lost all their mischief and went soft when he took in my smile. My chest squeezed and a lump formed in my throat. And, crap, there went that sting behind the bridge in my nose again!

It was second nature for me to get turned on by a guy eying me, but this was different. *So* different. It wasn't my lady bits that were clamoring for this man. It was my heart.

"Livvy? You still there?"

I swallowed past the lump and forced myself to breathe, but I didn't break eye contact with Brett.

"Yeah. Sorry. We'll be home in a minute."

One side of Brett's mouth tipped up just a touch before he caressed me with his gaze one last time and turned toward home.

It seemed my feelings weren't something I had any control over after all. I could try defining them all I wanted, but they weren't waiting for me. They'd decided to move straight past *open to possibilities* and on to *all-freaking-in.*

Gulp.

Six hours, one afternoon Guardians game, and ten sloppy hugs later, Haley packed up her bag and her dog and headed back to Wilmington. I still hated that we were apart, but it felt a little easier watching the taillights this time around. Something I had a hunch I could thank the man upstairs in my apartment for.

When I lost sight of Haley's car, I turned and bounded up the stairs to my apartment like it was Christmas morning and I'd been a really, *really* good girl.

I found Brett in conversation with Bo in my kitchen, and by that I mean Brett was petting my dog and Bo was staring up at him like he was the inventor of the squeak toy. He'd run home before the game for a shower and change of clothes and was wearing my favorite ripped jeans and another of his no-nonsense t-shirts—this one white. His beard was tidy again, but his hair was a mess, which was fine by me because I was planning on messing it up anyway. I watched my guys for a minute before Brett noticed me leaning against the wall and shot me one of his perfectly lopsided smiles.

"Hey. Did Haley get off okay?"

I nodded and took a step toward him and Bo. My dog ignored me, but that was okay because my focus was on the hot man in my kitchen. "You have a key, don't you?" My tone came out speculative.

Brett's head tilted, one hand still playing with Tambo's ear as the dog shamelessly shoved his head against it. "Uh, is this about your office, because despite what Officer Lunchbreak said, I can assure you I don't."

Officer Lunchbreak? Oh well, I couldn't process that one just now. Instead, I shook my head and took another step. "Not that kind of key."

"I'm afraid you lost me." He looked more amused than concerned.

"You have one of those keys to your heart. Or soul. Or inner being or whatever you want to call it."

"Ah." He let go of Bo and faced me fully. Bo grunted and sank to the tile at Brett's feet, clearly spent. Brett studied me and then nodded as if I didn't sound completely nuts. "That kind of key."

I nodded back and then frowned when his nod turned to a shake instead.

He shoved his hands in his pockets. "I'm afraid I don't, though."

Hmm. I really thought I'd figured this relationship shit out. I scratched my forehead. "Semantics." I waved a dismissive hand.

But he kept shaking his head. "Just because I don't have it doesn't mean there isn't one."

He was playing mind games with me. I pursed my lips, ready to tell him to drop his existential bullshit, but my retort died in my throat at his next words.

"I already gave it to *you*. You just have to decide if you want to use it."

And if that wasn't the biggest turn on ever in the history of the world, I'd give up baseball and horses too. My insides melted and my heart threatened to jump out of my chest and hand itself over to Brett complete with handcuffs for safekeeping. Apparently my heart was a kinky little thing.

I knew he was waiting for me to make the next move, so I took a deep breath and a step closer to him. Then one more until only Bo's big body separated us. "I never knew love could be so damn sexy."

His brows popped at the l-word.

I shrugged. "Well, you know what I mean."

He grinned, and I could have sworn I heard a faint *click* of a lock.

My heart raced double time and nervous tingles raced through my stomach. It was the Thursday after Brett and I had finally figured our shit out, and I swear I'd hardly slept that whole week. I was on some kind of euphoric high fueled by whatever it was Brett was doing to me—and I don't mean in the bedroom. Although we'd seen each other every night, we each retreated to our own places to sleep. Or toss and turn. Or make use of battery-powered personal items. But we hadn't slept together. Until tonight.

We'd just come back to my place after catching a high school baseball game where I met Jay—a.k.a. my favorite future major league pitcher. But when Brett pulled up to my place and walked me to the door, he followed me in instead of kissing me good-night like he'd been doing all week. That was his way of telling me that either we were done with the taking-it-slow approach or his penis had finally overtaken his brain and was now the official pilot of the mothership. Either way, I was good, but surprisingly nervous.

I'd never done this before. I mean, of course I'd had sex and I'd had boyfriends, but I'd never had true intimacy. I never wanted it with anyone before Brett. And the fact that he'd taken such care with our fledgling relationship made me want to hug him close and never let go. But I also wanted to have hot sweaty sex with him all night, so the hugs would have to wait a bit.

But, as always, Brett was going about things in his own way. In other words, he made himself comfortable on my couch and flipped on the TV, tuning it immediately to ESPN.

I decided to go with it and got us each a beer from the fridge before taking a seat next to him and handing his over.

"Thanks." That was it.

For the next hour, we watched hockey and some baseball highlights and drank our beers, neither of us even grazing the other with a finger. My pulse and nerves had all settled by the time *SportsCenter* came on.

Brett leaned forward to set his bottle and the remote on the coffee table and turned his attention to me. "Right. That should do it."

I hardly had time to deliver the look I reserved for weirdos before his arms were around me and he was kissing me like I'd just returned from war. I kissed him back with everything in me, sweeping my tongue into his mouth and reveling in the feel of his beard brushing my skin and his hands running their way down my sides and under the hem of my shirt.

I laughed into his mouth, finally figuring out what he'd been up to.

He pulled away for a few seconds and winked a naughty blue eye at me. "I could hear your brain working from the minute I walked in the door."

"Shut up."

"Yes, ma'am." He got back to the kissing thing and it was spectacular.

Before long, we'd both lost our shirts and moved to my bedroom where we had more space to work with and wouldn't have an audience, meaning we locked Tambo out. I was beginning to think my dog had a crush on Brett—not that I could blame him really. He was awfully good at the petting thing.

Next went my bra, which Brett tossed over his shoulder before taking his time exploring each of my breasts with his lips, teeth, tongue, and beard, whipping me up into a panting mess. Needing even more contact, I finally threw my leg over his hip and pressed my bare breasts against his chest, the contact making my nipples even harder if that was possible. Brett rolled to his back and pulled me over him and I didn't hesitate to grind down on his erection through the material of our clothes. God, he made me ache in such a fantastic way. I groaned into his mouth and he broke the kiss so we didn't die of asphyxiation. While we caught our breath, I sat up and traced the contours of his chest, pausing to brush a fingertip over his nipple. He shivered.

His voice was thick when he spoke. "You're incredible." His eyes roamed my face and I knew I was flushed with wet lips and lust-drunk eyes. "I can't believe how lucky I am."

My heart flipped over and so did my belly. Where did this guy come from and what took him so long?

I shook my head, fingers still wandering over his warm, taught flesh. "You can't say stuff like that and expect me to stay calm."

His lips quirked. "I don't want you calm anymore."

I shot him a sly grin. "Good."

My fingers went for the button on his jeans, but he brushed my hand aside and quickly shucked both his jeans and boxer briefs, leaving him gloriously naked under me. I sat back on his thighs and took him in with wide eyes. In addition to the lion tattoo and the one of a baseball surrounded by a tribal sun on his arms, Brett had one more surprise in store. Let's just say his ears weren't the only thing he'd had pierced. I swallowed hard and may have let out a little whimper. Holy mother of God.

He didn't utter a word, but his grin said it all for him. He was enjoying shocking the shit out of me tonight. But I didn't have long to consider it because the next thing I knew, he had me on my back and he was tugging my cutoffs down my thighs, leaving me in nothing but a black satin thong that did very little to protect my modesty—if I had any, that was.

"Christ," he murmured as he bent to place a kiss on each thigh. Then he parted them and I could feel his hot breath through the thin material. I squirmed and felt goosebumps rise on my skin. Before I could blink he was pushing the material aside and was right there using his tongue, fingers, and beard to drive me down-right insane. I climaxed within minutes, wondering why in the hell I ever dismissed all those women who swore by the beard in bed. I'd truly been missing out.

"Brett," I groaned, feeling boneless and spent. He pulled himself up to cover me, stopping along the way to covertly wipe his mouth on the sheets and trail kisses over my stomach and breasts. I pulled him in to kiss him, not minding in the least that the scent and taste of me still lingered. It was hot, actually. We were coming together in more ways than just physically, and there was no room for holding back.

I reached between us to feel him, wanting to explore his cock and his piercing. I was getting my second wind and feeling a little feisty. "Another drunken night out with your friends?" I ran my finger over the metal and he twitched in my hand.

He grinned in return and thrust into my grip. "No. That was a solo trip."

I squeezed him and he groaned, dipping to bury his face in my neck where he nuzzled and nipped at my skin. Everything this man did felt incredible and I needed to feel him inside me. When I told him as much, he froze all movement and I felt my mouth turn down. "What's wrong?"

He rose up slowly on his hands, his expression crestfallen. "I don't have a fucking condom."

I tilted my chin down and laughed. "I got it covered, Slugger."

He scowled at the moniker but didn't hesitate to grab a condom from my bedside table when I pointed the way. He applied it before I could protest, but I'd make sure I got to do the honors next time. I wanted to get up close and personal with all of Brett.

He removed my thong and settled over me with his elbows on the bed. His hands came up to frame my face and all traces of humor fled as we gazed at each other for a long minute before he aligned himself and began pressing into me. Part of me wanted to squirm at the sheer intimacy of the moment but the rest of me just wanted to cherish it.

"God, that feels unbelievable," I moaned as my head tilted back on the sheets and my hips rose. Holy shit. Then Brett pulled out almost completely before thrusting to the hilt and making me cry out.

There was no possible way God didn't take notice over the next fifteen minutes or so with as many times as I called out his name. But I figured he was the one who invented sex, so he probably didn't mind much. Suffice it to say Brett rocked my fucking world.

We began with a slow rhythm but it built in intensity as I met his thrusts and wound my legs around him. I eventually ended up on top of him, one hand to his chest as I rode him and that piercing did its job and did it well. I had two more orgasms by the time Brett finally gave in to his release and I collapsed on his chest in a sweaty heap. His cock was still hard and still inside me. I wanted to propose we stay that way forever, but I knew I'd get hungry eventually.

Brett's hands continued to caress my skin and I shivered at the contact. "I can't believe how good that was," he said into my hair.

I shifted so I could look into his face without expending an ounce more energy than strictly necessary. "Me either. I mean… damn."

He grinned. "Couldn't have said it better myself."

EPILOGUE

RETT

One Month Later

"I admit defeat." Liv's arm flopped over her eyes and she lay like a ragdoll on the bed next to me.

"Not everything is a competition, you know."

She peeked out from under her arm. "I'm sorry. Have you met me?"

I sent her a fake scowl and dragged my ass out of bed to the bathroom. She whistled at my naked ass but I ignored it.

Damn, this last month with Liv had been the best of my life— she got me in a way I never knew possible, and it was clear she felt the same about me. In fact, we were well on our way to becoming one of those disgusting couples who finished each other's sentences—except that we'd both vowed to break up if we ever became that annoying.

But we really were a perfect match, both in and out of the bedroom. She was so responsive and full of sexual energy, I'd been a bit afraid I wouldn't be able to keep up. But the fact that she'd just declared she'd never catch up to me in the orgasm-gifting department said I was holding my own.

I flipped on the bathroom light and checked out the unfamiliar shower before turning on the spray and testing the temperature.

We hadn't gotten nearly enough sleep the night before, having driven until late and checking into our hotel just before midnight. But it was an unwritten rule that you had to have sex if you were staying at a hotel, so we took one for the team, staying up late and waking early for another round for good measure. We were both exhausted but on that sexually driven high that lets you go without sleep—instead using your partner's touch to fuel you through the day.

"I started the shower," I called back to Liv. "If you're not in here in the next two minutes, I'm carrying you."

She laughed from the other room and I stepped up to the vanity where I'd stashed my personal items. A whole group of us had decided at the last minute to take a road trip to Baltimore to catch the Black Dogs playing the Devils at a Saturday game. Even Haley and the new guy I had yet to meet were there.

I glanced in the mirror and noticed a mark on my chest. When I went in for closer inspection, I found that Liv had been quite busy. I had a hickey on my chest, a bite mark on my shoulder, and a few scratches down my back. Nothing could have made me any fucking happier, and I was pretty certain I hadn't left Liv unmarked either. We were out of control, in the best possible way.

"Okay, I'm coming for you!" I shouted and turned around to stride back into the bedroom.

"Wait! Stop!" Liv yelled a second too late. I instinctively cupped my hands over my junk just before seeing Haley in the doorway to the adjoining hotel room. Her hand clapped over her eyes with enough force to cause some damage.

"Oh my God! I didn't see anything!"

I knew that to be patently untrue, but I was more than willing to pretend if she was.

"We'll meet you downstairs," Liv said before shutting the door and turning to me with raised eyebrows. She was wrapped in a bedsheet and looked like a sex goddess. "You know we're gonna talk about you later, right?"

I just nodded with resignation. "I'm aware."

Liv went to her bag and pulled out a t-shirt and knit shorts. I frowned and hooked a thumb over my shoulder. "What about the shower?" I'd really been looking forward to testing the acoustics with the way Liv tended to verbalize her pleasure during sex.

"No time." She slipped on the clothes, and when she forewent the undergarments, I smiled and approached, but she held her hands out. "You can't get me all hot. Everybody's meeting us downstairs for breakfast."

I frowned again, knowing I was being childish. "But I'm not done with you yet."

She grinned at my expression and went up on her toes to plant a kiss on my lips. "I'll make it up to you later. I promise."

When we got off the elevator in the lobby, Ari was waiting. She was dressed in a short denim skirt and tight t-shirt in black and red, the Black Dogs' colors. She wore a temporary team tattoo on her cheek. She also wore a knowing smile. "Well, well, well. If it isn't my next-door neighbors." Liv froze.

Although Ari had apologized up and down for the whole stadium bathroom thing and done her best to assure Liv she really wasn't a violent person, Liv was still a bit wary around her. I was sure it would wear off with time, but clearly we weren't there yet.

"Hey, Ari," Liv managed. "Nice tattoo."

"Thanks. I got one for you too. I'm just running up to my room to get them."

"Oh. That's sweet of you. Thanks." Liv's shoulders relaxed.

I grabbed Liv's hand and gave it a squeeze as Ari hopped on the elevator. "Where is everybody?"

Ari gestured with her chin. "Dining room around the corner."

"See you in a minute then." We stepped in the directions she'd indicated.

"Hey, Liv!" Ari's voice rang through the space. "I almost forgot."

I could see my girl cringe in my peripheral vision and I could only guess what was coming.

"God stopped by and said you can stop calling him. He got the message." Ari's cackle was only silenced when the steel doors slid shut.

I pressed my lips together to keep from laughing and Liv pulled her hand from mine. "I don't want to hear a word." Then she stalked to the dining room and I followed after, enjoying the view the whole way.

"Go, number 8!"

"Way to go, Martel!"

"Yes!!!"

"Unbelievable!!"

"You've got balls of steel, Martel!"

That last one was Liv.

It was the bottom of the sixth inning and Joey had just completed a double play, tagging the Devils' runner out after catching an impossible hard-hit line drive. The visiting fans were going nuts, us most of all. Liv was jumping around like a maniac and had even hugged Ari in her excitement.

We'd, of course, been watching Joey play on TV since he'd been called up to the Black Dogs in the middle of the series with the Lancers last month. But this was the first time we'd seen him play in person and it was better than I'd ever imagined. I couldn't begin to fathom what it felt like for Liv—and Joey!

He had scored us all great tickets for the game in Baltimore and we were lined up a few rows back from the visiting dugout. Emerson, Gavin, and Ari had driven up together the day before with a practically vibrating Jay. Liv had told Joey all about him and Joey arranged for a VIP treatment Friday afternoon where Jay got to meet some of the team and hang out. They were all decked out in their Black Dogs gear along with Haley and her guy, Ted. He seemed like a solid guy, if a bit quiet, so I was sure we'd get along.

We all calmed our asses down after Joey's phenomenal play and it wasn't long before the Black Dog's got their third out and the inning ended. On his way back to the dugout, Joey sent Liv a chin lift, cool as can be. That dude was good. Liv leaned into me and snort-laughed into my shirt.

I loved seeing her so happy. There had been some moments over the last month that cast a bit of a shadow over her usual sunny spirit. News had come that Troy was released after his nagging shoulder injury took a turn for the worse. In the wake of that, he and Joey had connected to do a little fence-mending where the entire story of the prescription drugs had finally come to light.

Troy had indeed been cheating on Liv, which still made me want to kick his ass, but the woman he'd been cheating with was particularly vile, it turned out. She sold Troy some cock-and-bull story about her mom being desperate for pain meds she couldn't afford. And it wasn't long before she convinced him to lift "just a little" hydrocodone from Liv's office. It snowballed from there, and once Troy realized he was in over his head, she was threatening to pin it all on him if he bolted. This certainly affected his performance on the field and explained more than a few things.

But he'd figured out how to get out in the end and keep Liv in the clear, for which I was grateful. He stole back everything he could, as well as any evidence pointing to the source of the drugs. And we knew the rest.

Karma, being the righteous bitch she is, may have interfered with Troy's career in light of his assholish behavior, but it didn't ignore the girlfriend either. Without the stash from Troy, she'd apparently gotten sloppy and been arrested a couple weeks later.

Last Joey had heard, Troy was back home in Kansas looking for work. Liv tried to act like the whole thing was old news, but it was a reminder to all of us to take care of what we had and not take it for granted.

"First batter's up!" Liv bounced in her seat and poked me, breaking me out of my thoughts.

The Black Dog's right fielder approached the plate and adjusted his grip as the Devils' pitcher kneaded the ball, his eyes darting back and forth between the batter and catcher. When the pitcher released the ball, it appeared to cross the plate low and a bit outside but the ump called a strike.

Liv was out of her seat in a heartbeat. "You've got to be kidding me, ump!"

Ari leaned around Liv and gave me wide eyes. I just grinned at her. My woman was on a mission and I was enjoying the shit out of it. When Ari frowned back at me, I was about to reassure her that I had Liv covered when I realized she wasn't frowning at me. I turned to look behind me and saw Jax fucking Crosby standing at the end of our row, hands on his hips and his eyes pinning Ari in place.

Gavin, who was sitting on my other side, turned to see what we were looking at. "Hey, I didn't know Jax was coming."

I glanced back at Ari who had pulled her phone out and was pretending she didn't see him, thumbs working away and a casual expression parked on her face.

"I don't think anyone did," I replied.

Oblivious, Gavin raised a hand to greet our newcomer, but he only had eyes for Ari. And his eyes were not those of a happy man. This was disturbing for a number of reasons, the primary one being that Jax was both the shrewdest and most laid-back guy I'd ever met. Whatever had happened to get him into this kind of state must have been pretty damn big.

"Ariana!" He bellowed down the row and all of us except Ari turned his way.

"Jax, hey!" Emerson called, just as oblivious as her boyfriend.

Liv took a break from berating the umpire to look down at Ari. "I think that guy's trying to get your attention."

"*I* think that guy can go to hell for all I care," was her response.

Liv's wide eyes shot to me. "Uh, okay."

"Ariana!" He wasn't giving up, feet firmly planted and his blond hair sticking up in every direction.

Ari huffed and lowered her phone to her lap. "Oh, for the love of God." Then she got up out of her seat and we made room for her to pass. She pointed at Jax. "I'm only giving in to keep you from embarrassing the hell out of me. Remember that."

Jax dipped his chin and scanned her face before gesturing for her to precede him up the steps.

"What the hell was that all about?" Gavin asked.

I just shook my head, happy in my ignorance of the details.

"Here comes Joey!" Liv's voice brought our attention back to the field. Pitcher, batter, and catcher all went through their usual routines and it was only moments before a slider came careening across the plate. Joey swung and just missed, causing groans to ripple through our little crowd.

"That's okay, Martel! You're just keeping him on his toes!"

I looked up at Liv, her hands cupped around her gorgeous mouth and one of her numerous Black Dogs t-shirts hugging her body and making me want to haul her back to the hotel. I settled for placing my hand on her lower back instead.

She glanced down at me with a nervous smile. The second pitch was a ball, as was the third, but the next one was a wickedly sweet curveball—one that connected with Joey's bat and had him safe on first within seconds. We all cheered and Liv shed her nerves again.

But when our next batter hit a grounder that had Joey tagged out at second, Liv resurrected the crazy and directed it toward the second base ump.

"He was safe! What's the matter with you? Were you busy picking daisies or did you forget your seeing-eye dog at home?!"

Gavin snickered beside me and Emerson covered her mouth while Haley rolled her eyes playfully. I didn't see Jay's reaction, but I was guessing he was too focused on the game to even hear Liv.

"Ma'am." A voice came from beside the dugout just in front of us. One of the official umpire crew stood looking straight at my girlfriend.

I stood in the blink of an eye and put a hand up. "Sorry, sir. She
—" but Liv cut me off.

"I'll behave. I promise." She waved at the official and he
turned back to the field.

She pulled me down with her to our seats. "This is one game
I'm not getting kicked out of. I'll just squeeze your hand when I
feel the heckling coming on."

And she was as good as her word. By the ninth inning, the
Black Dogs were up by three, Liv was smiling bright, and every
bone in my right hand had been crushed to dust. But I didn't care.

I loved that Liv threw herself into everything she did, her
enthusiasm contagious. I loved that she didn't apologize for who
she was but was the first to admit to her own faults. And I loved
that she was willing to open herself up to love, even if it
scared her.

And when Joey crossed over home plate to score his first
homerun in the majors, I loved that she was happier for him than
anyone else in the entire damn stadium.

I sat back in my seat, listening to her cheer long after the play
was over as a satisfied smile settled itself on my lips. My eyes
went to the field and the blue afternoon sky. It was a perfect
summer day. Friends, baseball, sunshine, and my girl at my side.
What could be better than that?

~THE END~

Up next is Ari and Jax's story in **The Runaround**.
And don't forget to grab your copy of **The Nerd Next Door**, Haley
and Ted's story in the spin-off series called *Carolina Kisses*.
Turn the page for excerpts.

Stay up to date on Sylvie's upcoming books and projects by subscribing to her newsletter! http://bit.ly/NewsSylvie

www.sylviestewartauthor.com

Want to hear the dirt from Sylvie about *The Way You Are*? Check out **Sylvie Says** after the excerpts.

ALSO BY SYLVIE STEWART

The Fix (*Carolina Connections* Book 1)

The Spark (*Carolina Connections* Book 2)

The Lucky One (*Carolina Connections* Book 3)

The Game (*Carolina Connections* Book 4)

The Runaround (*Carolina Connections* Book 6)

The Nerd Next Door (*Carolina Kisses,* Book 1)

New Jerk in Town (*Carolina Kisses,* Book 2)

The Last Good Liar (*Carolina Kisses*, Book 3)

Between a Rock and a Royal (*Kings of Carolina, Book* 1)

Blue Bloods and Backroads (*Kings of Carolina, Book* 2)

Stealing Kisses With a King (*Kings of Carolina*, Book 3)

Game Changer

Happy New You

Then Again

About That

Full-On Clinger (*Love on Tap* novella/prequel)

Booby Trapped (Asheville short)

Crushing on Casanova (Asheville short)

Taunted (Asheville short)

Love on Tap Series - coming 2022

EXCERPT FROM THE RUNAROUND

Carolina Connections, Book 6 (Ari and Jax)

Chapter Two

JAX

"Don't even think about it, asshole," I muttered into my empty beer bottle before dropping it back to the bartop, completely disgusted with myself. She had me turned so inside out I was sucking on an empty beer, for Christ's sake. My eyes stayed on her full ass until she swung it around the corner and all I had was the sweet memory of it to keep me company.

Ariana Amante had a way of fucking with my mind, even when she didn't mean to. Not that I didn't see the clear delight in her eyes when she purposely challenged me—which was often. And, every damn time, it made me hard—something I should have remembered before I hunted her down tonight. My dick was gonna have zipper marks tattooed on it if I didn't get the hell out of here.

I flagged down the bartender, the same one who'd been sending Ariana puppy eyes all night, and asked for the check.

"I got hers. You can pay for yours," the kid said.

I gave him my best *no-fuckin'-way* glare and held up a twenty between my fingers before dropping it on the bar between us. "This'll cover both." Then I pushed back from the bar and walked off before he could respond. I couldn't blame the kid for panting after Ariana. She was every man's wet dream with her golden-bronze skin, long, silky hair and banging body with more curves than a Formula One circuit. But he didn't stand a chance in hell with a girl like her. She *played* with boys, this much I knew already.

I'd considered letting her try her game on me then showing her what it was like to date a *man* for a change, but that was before— before I'd gotten myself into a cluster the likes of which hadn't been seen since Pete Rose decided to give gambling a try.

And that right there was how I'd found my nearly forty-year-old self crashing a karaoke party at a shit bar downtown full of drunk kids and lovesick bartenders. Yeah, that was about on par for how things had been going lately for Jax Crosby.

Now, I pride myself on not letting shit get to me, but damn if God wasn't laughing like the devil himself at my ass lately. But I had a plan, as usual—one designed to return my life to its comfortable normal and rid myself of this unsettled feeling that had become my constant companion these last months. That meant regaining control and keeping complications to a minimum.

It also meant this wasn't the right moment to give the time or inclination to taking on an experiment like Ariana. Because that's what it would have been—an experiment. Nothing more.

No, I just needed her to do me this favor and then I could forget all about her again. Women came and went, just like everything else, and there was plenty of shit waiting on the other side of town and at my office that needed my time more than my dick needed to get laid. With that in mind, I steered my ass to the door, telling myself it was time to go.

Ariana's voice stopped me with my hand to the wood paneled door.

"Let's start this hour off with one of my favorites, shall we?" She teased the audience with her throaty laugh. "I'm sure you all know this one, so feel free to sing along."

The first few notes of Aretha Franklin's "Natural Woman" flowed from the speakers and I couldn't have stopped myself from turning around for anything.

Hardly a single person in the entire damn place uttered a sound as she launched into the first verse, her velvety tone hitting me in the gut like a sucker punch. I was captivated, standing there like a fool with my hand on the door and my head and nuts trying their best to bust out of me and jump on stage. How she was singing in a dive bar in Greensboro, North Carolina, instead of up on a stage at some packed stadium was beyond me.

I didn't know much about music, but I knew enough to be certain that Ariana Amante had something that didn't come along often. Her red painted lips slid into a sultry smile when she hit the chorus while one hand skimmed down over her waist and hip like a lover's touch, making my inner caveman clench his teeth and demand I march right up to the stage and carry her over my shoulder and out of this shithole. But to what end?

Yeah, I needed to stick to the plan and stay focused. And that meant getting my ass home.

Allowing myself one last drink of her lush body in that temptation of a black dress, I exhaled and pushed through the door. Her voice followed me for half a block until the street sounds drowned it out and I was back in my familiar world on my own. Hands shoved in my pockets, I bowed my head to the light spring drizzle and walked to my truck.

I'd have to steel myself before our next encounter. There was no room for getting reeled in by her siren call. Not happening.

One thing was for sure, though. Lola hadn't been lying when she said Ariana was the best singer she'd ever heard. And, damn, if that wasn't inconvenient as hell.

Get your copy of *The Runaround* to continue reading Ari and Jax's story!
Also available in audiobook and e-book

EXCERPT FROM THE NERD NEXT DOOR

(Carolina Kisses #1 - Haley and Ted)

Chapter One: *Game On*

HALEY

"Do you think I'm overreacting?" I speed my steps to catch up. "I mean, it's not like he tried to feel me up or anything, but I just got that skeevy vibe. You know what I mean?" My nose scrunches as I think about my last client of the day—or should I say, the *owner* of my last client of the day?

"Are you even listening?" I stop short, causing Tank to halt as well. He turns his brown eyes to me and gets that wrinkly little crease between his brows. His head cocks to the side and I bend to pet him. "Of course you were. Sorry to doubt you."

I straighten and take a quick look around to make sure no one is witnessing the crazy lady talking to her dog about creepy dudes, but the pathway is empty except for my mutt and me. The air is sticky and I can feel the boob sweat forming, but Tank and I both need our exercise so I start down the pavement once more. Trees line either side of the path, making the surroundings much more pleasant than the exhaust-choked sidewalks we used to walk when I was still in school in Richmond. Tank and I both prefer our new home in Wilmington. The park is only a few minutes' walk from our apartment and we're close to the beach, which is a huge bonus. Now, if we could just make some friends.

"But not Mr. Nemeth!" I tell Tank, as if he'd suggested I try making nice with that creepy client from this afternoon.

As the newbie at Coastal Veterinary Clinic, it fell on me to take the Saturday shift, which I normally wouldn't mind. But add a perv into the mix and I was wishing someone else had been in the mood to work the weekend in my place.

My first clue that I was dealing with a good-old-fashioned dirtbag was the position of his eyes. When I walked into the clinic room, cheery smile in place, I found the man sitting on the bench staring directly at my boobs while he stroked his calico. And, no, that's not a euphemism.

Even when I said hello and introduced myself, his eyes took a good long while to rise to my face. Ugh. And, don't get me wrong, I'm all about loving on our furry friends, but when a dude is clearly envisioning you naked while running his fingers rhythmically through an animal's hair, it's time to back away slowly. Unfortunately, my job wouldn't allow that. His cat had an upset stomach, and I was the vet assigned to poor Ariana Grande Latte. Yes, that is the cat's name.

"So, it sounds like your cat is having tummy troubles." I set the patient file on the high countertop and motioned for the guy to settle his feline on the fuzzy mat.

He cleared his throat and stood, still stroking the cat and making me clench my teeth so I didn't say anything unprofessional. He approached and leaned much farther than strictly necessary over the counter to deposit the cat. I forced myself not to jump back or smack him on the head.

"Uh, yeah. She can't seem to keep any food down." He finally released the cat and I waited for him to straighten before scratching her on her soft little head. She was a gorgeous long-haired calico with bright blue eyes and a crooked tail, which just made her more beautiful in my eyes. I'm a sucker for unique traits and idiosyncrasies that make each animal special.

"Hey there, sweetie. I hear you're not feeling well." I rolled her over and prodded gently at her abdomen. "Did you notice anything she may have gotten into? I see she's declawed, so I assume she's an indoor cat?" When he didn't answer right away, I looked up to see that his eyes had gone kind of lazy and were following my hands as they moved over his pet. Uh, eww. "Possibly something in the garage?"

The man shook his head and finally looked back up. "Not that I can think of..." He paused and made a show of checking out my name tag—which just happened to rest over my right boob. "... Haley."

I wanted to roll my eyes and then take a hot bleach shower. I suppose he wasn't unattractive in an objective sense. Average height, muscular build, wide-set eyes, and blond hair covered in a baseball cap. But he had creeper written all over him. Call it a gut feeling. And my gut was telling me to wrap this shit up.

He watched me check the cat's gums and listen to her back and abdomen with my stethoscope. But I couldn't determine anything without some tests. I looped the scope around my neck again and took a step back, putting my hands in the pockets of my white coat and firmly out of his view. He licked his bottom lip and I was D-O-N-E, done.

"Well, Mr. Nemeth, we'll need to collect a stool sample. Do you think you can get your cat to defecate for us?"

His head snapped down to Ariana Grande Latte. Yup. That did it.

Tank and I stop at the cross street that intersects the park trail. He sits on his doggy behind and mimics me by looking both ways before we cross over to the other side. He's a good boy like that. With the live oaks and flowering bushes surrounding us again we have our nice little cocoon of shade and sweet-smelling air, but it's time to head home and figure out dinner. My mutt still hasn't taken care of business but I'm giving up. He has a habit of waiting until the last possible moment, and I suspect it's all part of a plan to trick me into longer walks. Not that my ass couldn't use it, but I'm exhausted from the work day.

"Come on, dude. We're going home." I could swear I hear him grunt, but he follows my lead as I cut through a lightly worn dirt path along the side of the walkway. A branch scratches my arm and Tank kicks up a cloud of dust, making a bath for both of us a necessity. We emerge by the apartment complex, and I'm just about to scold my mutt for making a mess when I stop dead in my tracks.

Pulling up to our building in a dark blue late-model Mazda is the object of my... fascination? Obsession? Slightly stalkerish tendencies? *Jesus.* Who's the creeper now? The car settles in a spot by the curb, the driver's side door opening shortly after. And out steps Ted Jones. *My* Ted Jones. Well, he would be if I had my way about it.

I tilt my head to the side and admire him for a moment or two. Now, here's a man who knows how to rock an elbow patch. *Oooh, yeah.* I don't know what it is about Ted Jones' particular brand of nerdiness, but it is friggin' hot. I've done a little, let's call it...

investigating and discovered he teaches in the liberal arts school at NCUW, so I know he's whip smart. He also wears the sexiest black-framed glasses over brilliant blue eyes, has little to no affection for his razor, and exercises a habit of smoothing his hair down to fight a stubborn cowlick. It never obeys, much to my delight, making him sport a constant just-rolled-out-of-bed look.

In contrast to that, he is always dressed neatly, often in a traditional tweed jacket with elbow patches which he pairs with jeans that do amazing things for his ass. Something about that combination of tweed, leather, and denim sets off an odd Pavlovian response in my uterus. I can't explain it. To top that all off, he's a runner, and I've seen the muscles of his thighs and calves bunching as he powers through his evening runs, leaving him coated in sweat and me with plenty to think about when my head hits the pillow.

It's safe to say I'm gone over Ted Jones.

The only problem is we've never actually had a single conversation.

To be fair, we *have* spoken to one another—on several occasions, in fact. But you couldn't exactly call these interactions conversations. As I recall, my first word to him was, "Hi." To which I got zero reply.

It was the afternoon I moved into my apartment, the unseasonably cool temperatures making my fingers sore from cold. I'd just returned a borrowed cart to maintenance and was trying to remember which walkway would take me to my building when I got my first glimpse of my future boyfriend (positive thinking is always recommended). Although, to be honest, it was the teenage girl speaking to him who first caught my attention and caused me to do a double take.

The two stood on the sidewalk while the brisk early-spring temperatures caused us all to tighten our coats around us. When I first saw the girl, I could have sworn a bag of cotton candy rested on her head—the classic dual pack with sugary clouds of half pink and half blue. But, no, it was just her hair, so my attention quickly shifted to take in the man beside her.

He wore a dark wool coat and I could see the puffs of his breath on the air as he laughed at something the girl showed him. It was a magazine of some sort, called *The Weatherman*, although I'd never heard of it. Both the girl and man were seemingly enthralled and neither one noticed me as my insides turned to mush. His laughter skipped toward me on the breeze and made my stomach flip—and this was before I'd ever even seen him in his tweed, denim, and leather trifecta of hotness.

The two spoke animatedly, the girl gesturing with wide sweeps of her arms as her cotton-candy hair swished around her ears. He flipped some pages until he found what he was looking for and they both buried their noses—and every other sense, it seemed—into the magazine. I felt oddly left out, even though I'd never laid eyes on either of these people before in my life. After a few moments, I stole one last look and retreated down the cement walkway to what I was almost certain was my building.

So it was no surprise that I all but gasped when I found myself on the elevator of my apartment building not two hours later with the very same man—sans teenage girl this time. I mean, what were the chances of him living in the same building as me in such a huge complex? It was clearly a sign, as was the uptick in my heart rate as I got my first close-up view of him. I drew in a breath and uttered my very first word.

"Hi." Yes, I am available to teach flirting lessons should anyone need my brilliant advice.

He didn't even glance my way. Here I was in an enclosed space with this delicious guy who immediately pushed all my buttons—

making me want to push the emergency button on the elevator and make out with him in a really dirty way—and he wouldn't even acknowledge me.

I've never been great with guys, but I do okay. Certainly well enough to spark up a casual conversation in an elevator. When he left me hanging, I felt a sharp pang that this guy who was friendly to *Weatherman* girls and was my type in every way was actually kind of a rude jerk. That was, until I noticed he was wearing some of those weird wireless earbuds. This discovery brought some relief, but I still stood awkwardly until we reached the third floor where I got off.

Refusing to concede defeat, I waited until the elevator was about to close behind me and turned to give him my best smile and a friendly wave. Unfortunately, I missed the small fact that he had stepped out after me. Which meant when I whipped myself around, my forehead made audible contact with his very defined cheekbone, causing us both to stagger back.

"I'm so sorry!" I put one hand to my head and one out toward him, as if my hand held a magical power that dulled the pain from blunt-force trauma.

He held his cheek and blinked a few times, his jaw working as if to test the level of injury. Then he pulled out an earbud and shook his head, his gaze dropping to the floor.

His voice was a deep, quiet rumble when he spoke. "No problem."

Then he snatched a set of keys from his pocket like he thought I might attack again and made quick work of the lock to apartment 3-C. The apartment right next to my 3-B. Ack!

"Happens all the time," he mumbled before disappearing behind his door. I continued to stand in the hallway, unsure of what had just happened and wondering if I should run to the store for some frozen peas or something. But I got the distinct feeling that would just make things more awkward.

Little did I know, awkward would be our go-to vibe for all subsequent encounters.

Like the time my grocery bag split and a bottle of wine, a huge roll of chocolate-chip cookie dough, and a box of panty liners came tumbling out at his feet. Instead of just picking them up like a normal person, I, for some unknown reason, felt compelled to share that I was PMSing.

Because that's exactly the topic that's gonna make your crush confess his undying love for you. *Oh, Haley, there's nothing I find sexier than the mental image of you stuffing your panties with cotton personal products before binge drinking and shoving raw cookie dough in your face. Come to daddy!*

Yeah. That's pretty much how things have gone since.

But not today! Today, I'm going to have a real live conversation with Ted Jones.

I straighten my back and then glance down at my clothes. The old t-shirt and capri leggings can't be helped. I take a quick sniff in the general direction of my armpits and resolved to just keep my arms glued to my sides during the course of our scintillating discussion. Hell, he's a runner. Maybe he's into girls who work up a sweat.

I stride forward, pulling Tank along as I watch Ted stop at the communal mailboxes on a grassy patch of lawn. He stands with his back to me, his legs shoulder width apart and covered in the familiar denim.

I can do this. I'll be confident and charming and not even a little bit weird—I'm sure of it. That is, until I actually reach the mailboxes and catch Ted's scent. Lordy, he smells like pencil shavings and leather. I want to bite my fist and then lick his neck.

Instead, I pretend to search for my mailbox key which I know to be sitting in a dish on my entry table at this very moment.

Ted doesn't turn his head or acknowledge me in any way. He closes his mailbox and removes his key before sifting through the stack of white envelopes and coupon fliers.

It's now or never. I take a deep breath and turn to him, one hand on my hip and the other gripping the plastic handle of Tank's leash. "Beautiful evening, huh?"

Dammit! *The weather? Seriously?* I'm a walking cliché, but it's too late, so I widen my smile. Ted turns to me and, upon taking in my overly enthusiastic smile, takes a step back.

Right into the pile of shit my dog just dropped behind him.

Get your copy of ***The Nerd Next Door*** to continue reading Haley and Ted's story!

SYLVIE SAYS

Let's Get Real about The Way You Are

I love this story for so many reasons, but I think mostly because Brett is the precise opposite of a typical romance-book hero. He's not the alpha, he's not the most popular guy in town, he's not the hottest guy out there—or the most coordinated, he was never a star athlete, he's never in his life had a little black book. He's just Brett. And he's unapologetic about that. Which makes him AWESOME.

Brett also has the worst potty mouth of the whole Carolina Connections gang, but I tried my best not to overdo it. He just has this way of throwing out those f-bombs, though!

I hope you guys were rooting for him throughout the book as much as I was. And I know I was totally mean by putting the kibosh on the sex when Liv was ready to jump him. Sorry, not sorry.

Liv is my girl because she speaks her mind, she's impulsive, and she's not afraid of a challenge. Her career is kick-ass and she's smart as a whip. Liv may dive into life, but she's cautious with her heart. She's also her own worst enemy at times, which I think so many of us are.

I want to be like Liv in a lot of ways, but I've never been cautious with my heart—I tend to throw it out there like candy at a damn parade! But, hey, you only live once, right?

Sex: Liv is a horny girl and she does not apologize for it. I *needed* her in the series! Of course, Brett isn't exactly a low-testosterone kind of guy, but he wants that emotional connection (Awwww). But I think Brett get the last laugh with the nice little surprise hiding in his boxer briefs, don't you?

Tambo: Book boyfriends are great, but book dogfriends are amazing too. I want to snuggle up with Bo and use him as a pillow.

Olivia Newton-John: I know it may seem random, but it's not, I promise you. I used to love, love, love her when I was a kid and a teenager—and, *fine*, I still love her. I mean, what girl (born before 1985, that is) didn't watch Grease three hundred times, each viewing from the vantage point of someone's living-room floor with ten of her best friends nestled up next to her in puffy sleeping bags? And our parents must have thought we were clueless idiots when we danced around singing "Let's Get Physical," all the while thinking ONJ was talking about working up a sweat at the gym. You got us good, Ms. Newton-John.

The Friend Zone: Yeah, it sucks, but sometimes showing someone who you are through the lens of friendship can lead to the best outcome. For some people, they find love elsewhere but still have a good friend to show for it. For others, like Brett and Liv, it can become the foundation for an amazing love connection.

I really hope you fell in love with Brett and Liv and enjoyed touching base with the whole gang!

Now for what's up next. Liv's bestie, Haley, has her own book

(*The Nerd Next Door*), so don't miss out! The newest addition to the Carolina Connections series is LIVE!! *The Runaround* will to steal your heart and ignite your panties! (Think hot single dad, Jax, meets independent singer, Ari)

Also, if you haven't read the first four books in the Carolina Connections series, you must go do that now! But I've got tons of other stuff coming up too, so you'll want to sign up for my newsletter and/or join my Facebook group for sure. I make new plans all the time in my little author world and you don't want to miss anything.

Here's a short list of what's going on:

- The first book in my new *Love on Tap* series comes out Summer 2022! And, of course, it takes place in North Carolina. This time it's in the amazing town of Asheville, and it involves hot brothers and kick-ass women. You can read the prequel now in *Full-On Clinger*.
- Liv's cousin, Joey Martel, is getting his own book in the *Carolina Connections* series.
- Almost ALL my books are now available in audio so you definitely want to check them out!
- I have another charity anthology with my romcom author friends coming out this holiday season, so keep an eye out.
- Ollie will have his own story but I haven't decided where it fits in yet. It's gonna be a little different than my usual romcoms.
- *Did you know you get a* **FREE** *e-book when you sign up for my newsletter?* www.sylviestewartauthor.com

That's it for now… You guys are amazing, and I'm so incredibly thankful to have you as READERS! There would be no books without you, so thanks from the bottom of my heart!

XOXO,

Sylvie

ABOUT THE AUTHOR

Sylvie Stewart is a *USA Today* bestselling author of romantic comedy and contemporary romance. She's married to a hilarious dude and has crazy twin boys who keep her busy and make her world go 'round. Her love of all things North Carolina is no secret, nor is her ultimate wish of snuggling her very own pet baby goat. If you love smart Southern gals, hot blue-collar guys, and snort-laughing with characters who feel like your best friends, Sylvie's your gal.

Want to stay updated on all things Sylvie?
Subscribe to my newsletter! http://bit.ly/NewsSylvie

Want to hang out with me and my readers?
Join my reader group on Facebook: **Sylvie's Spot - for the Sexy, Sassy, and Smartassy!** http://facebook.com/groups/SylviesSpot

Thanks! XOXO,
Sylvie

Keep up to date and keep in touch!
www.sylviestewartauthor.com

sylvie@sylviestewartauthor.com

facebook.com/SylvieStewartAuthor
twitter.com/sylvie_stewart_
instagram.com/sylvie.stewart.romance
bookbub.com/authors/sylvie-stewart
pinterest.com/sylviestewartauthor

ACKNOWLEDGMENTS

As always, I need to send a big thanks to my friend and editor, Heather Mann, and to my hubby and kids for all their patience when I say, "Just five more minutes," only to emerge from my office thirty minutes later.

Thank you to all my friends in the indie author world… there are so many of you I can't possibly name you all, but I am proud to be a member of a community that's so nurturing and generous. I do need to give a special shout out to my PA, Lea who is so very good at saving my ass, and to all the bloggers out there who work tirelessly to promote our work to readers. Special thanks to the ever-inspiring and ever-patient Krista, as well as Rebecca, Monica, and all the box set leaders I worked with this year. And I need to holler at my RomCom pals and the whole crew at IAS. You are all AMAZING!

And, lastly, none of this would be possible without my readers!! Thank you so much for buying and reading my stories, and for your messages, feedback, and rants about the jerks in my books. You make all the hard work worth it!

Made in the USA
Las Vegas, NV
09 March 2023

68776428R00125